THE FORTUNES OF TEXAS

*Follow the lives and loves of a wealthy family
with a rich history and deep ties
in the Lone Star State*

THE HOTEL FORTUNE

Check in to the Hotel Fortune,
the Fortune brothers' latest venture
in cozy Rambling Rose, Texas. They're
scheduled to open on Valentine's Day, when
a suspicious accident damages a balcony—
and injures one of the workers!
Now the future of the hotel could be
in jeopardy. *Was* the crash an accident—
or is something more nefarious going on?

Charismatic Brady Fortune is perfectly suited
to his job as concierge at the Hotel Fortune.
And he knows he has caught the attention
of his new nanny, Harper Radcliffe. She seems
to see the vulnerability beneath his confident
swagger. And she's the only one who
can contain the rambunctious twins who
are suddenly his. Falling for Harper seems like
a *really* bad idea. Or it could be the
best worst thing he ever does...

THE FORTUNES OF TEXAS: The Hotel Fortune

Dearest Reader,

This page is normally devoted to the world that a particular book revolves around, be it one that encompasses a specific limited series or one of the worlds I have been fortunate enough to be allowed to create and write about. However, as I work on attempting to make yet another chapter within the vast Fortune family come to life, right now the actual world around me—not just the country I was lucky enough to emigrate to with my mother and father all those years ago, but the entire *world*—is struggling to survive as everyone attempts to weather this never-experienced-before storm, praying that the sun will come out, if not tomorrow then in the foreseeable, near future. I truly believe it will and that we will all be the stronger and, possibly, the wiser for it.

In the meantime, I am doing my part by remaining positive and trying my very best to entertain you by diverting your attention for the short while that it takes to read this book. And in diverting you, I am also succeeding in diverting myself. I see it as a win-win situation.

As always, I thank you for reading one of my books, and from the bottom of my heart, I wish you someone to love who loves you back.

One final word in closing. Remember, we're all in this together and we shall make it into the light— *together.*

All my love,

Marie Ferrarella

An Unexpected Father

MARIE FERRARELLA

HARLEQUIN

SPECIAL EDITION

Special thanks and acknowledgment are given
to Marie Ferrarella for her contribution to the
The Fortunes of Texas: The Hotel Fortune miniseries.

Recycling programs
for this product may
not exist in your area.

ISBN-13: 978-1-335-40471-8

An Unexpected Father

Copyright © 2021 by Harlequin Books S.A.

This edition published by arrangement with Harlequin Books S.A.

For questions and comments about the quality of this book, please contact us at CustomerService@Harlequin.com.

Harlequin Enterprises ULC
22 Adelaide St. West, 40th Floor
Toronto, Ontario M5H 4E3, Canada
www.Harlequin.com

Printed in U.S.A.

USA TODAY bestselling and RITA® Award–winning author **Marie Ferrarella** has written more than two hundred and fifty books for Harlequin, some under the name Marie Nicole. Her romances are beloved by fans worldwide. Visit her website, marieferrarella.com.

To

All the Target and Grocery Store Clerks

Who Came In During the Coronavirus Pandemic

So We Could Shop and Buy Food

You Kept Me Sane

Thank You!

Prologue

This had to be a dream, Brady Fortune told himself. A really bad dream.

No, not a dream, he amended.

A nightmare.

And any second now, he was going to wake up and everything would be just the way it was supposed to be. Life would be back to normal.

But it wasn't back to normal. It would never be back to normal again

Brady felt completely numb, from his stunned, frozen heart, right down to his very toes.

It took him a moment to realize that he was clutching his outdated cell phone so hard, it was perilously close to being snapped in half.

Breathe, damn it, Brady. Breathe!

The simple directive throbbed over and over again in his head. He drew in a deep breath, then let it out. His heart continued racing at an uncontrollable pace. He drew in another deep breath, but that didn't help either.

His heart was still pounding like a bass drum.

"Mr. Fortune? Mr. Fortune, are you still there?" Brady heard a faraway voice on his cell phone asking him. The deep voice corkscrewed its way deep into his consciousness.

It was the voice of Allen Mayfair, Gord and Gina's lawyer. The man who had just sent his entire world reeling before it burst into flames.

"Yes, I'm still here." Brady heard a voice that sounded a lot like his own answering the lawyer's question. It took him another couple of moments to realize that the hollow, stunned voice he heard actually belonged to him. Brady tried again. "Yes, I'm still here," he repeated more firmly.

"I realize that this must be such a shock to you. I am really sorry to be the bearer of such terrible news, Mr. Fortune," the lawyer was saying.

Five minutes ago everything had been fine. And then his phone rang. Mayfair was calling to break the worst possible news to him: that his best friend, Gordon, and Gord's wife, Gina, had been killed in a horrific motorcycle accident.

He refused to believe it.

He had to believe it.

Brady was realistic enough to know that life was about terrible things happening, terrible things that were hiding in the shadows, ready to just jump out at you at the worst possible time.

As if there was *ever* a good time for something like this to happen.

"No," the voice on the other end of the call assured him. "They didn't suffer. It was instantaneous."

He knew he should have been comforted by that, but he wasn't. Wasn't because he knew he wouldn't ever hear Gord's deep voice calling him up to *get off your duff because we've got things to do and places to see*. Never hear his best friend's oddly high-pitched laugh again when something struck him as being weirdly funny.

Never see Gord again or do any of the things they had made plans to do ever since they were kids.

"Mr. Fortune? Did you hear my question?"

No, he hadn't. His mind had gone elsewhere. "Wh-what?"

Brady realized that he had gotten lost in his thoughts again, silently railing at Gord for being such a thoughtless fool as to go riding on a motorcycle like that when he had little kids to think of.

Little kids who were all alone now.

"No, I'm sorry. I didn't," Brady apologized.

"Could you repeat what you just said?" He hadn't a clue as to what the lawyer had just said and he wasn't up to trying to pretend that he knew.

Mayfair patiently repeated his question. "I asked how soon you think that you could come by to pick up the twins?"

"The twins?" Brady repeated numbly, his brain incapable of processing the question or making any sense of it.

Nothing was making any sense to him anymore.

"Yes, the twins," the lawyer repeated, then added in the boys' names as if that would clear everything up. "Toby and Tyler. Gordon and Gina's children."

"Why would I be picking them up?" Brady wanted to know, confused.

He wasn't all that good with kids. Had Gord thought he could somehow comfort the twins if something awful were to happen to him and his wife—which it had, Brady thought angrily. Brady's eyes stung as he blinked back tears. Gord knew him better than that.

"Wouldn't they be better off with one of Gina's relatives? Or Gord's parents?" Anyone but him, Brady thought. He was in need of comforting himself. He wasn't in any position to offer it.

"Apparently they didn't think so. As I told you, Mr. and Mrs. Jefferson named you as their twins' legal guardian in their will."

"Legal guardian," Brady repeated. Obviously, he'd missed that part of the conversation.

"Yes. That means that you are now completely responsible for Toby and Tyler," the lawyer patiently explained.

"You mean for now?" Brady asked, trying to get his bearings. This had to be some kind of temporary arrangement until the actual guardian or guardians for the twins could come for them.

This was all so surreal. His head was still swirling as fragments of thoughts continued to chase one another through his brain.

"No, permanently," Mayfair told him. His voice indicated that he was rather confused as to why the man he was speaking to would have thought the arrangement for the twins' guardianship was only temporary.

And just like that, with those words, Brady's whole life was completely and indelibly changed forever.

Chapter One

Six months later...

Looking back, it seemed rather incredible how much time had somehow managed to go by since his friends' deaths. Six months since he had become an instant father. Six long, grueling, painful months and if anything, Brady felt more lost than ever in this new role he had assumed.

He hadn't even had time to properly grieve over the loss of his best friend. The moment he walked in the door from work during the week, not to mention the whole of the entire weekend, Brady was too busy chasing after two overly-energized four-year-olds. Four-year-olds whose batteries never seemed to run down or need even a minimum of recharging.

From the moment Toby and Tyler opened their eyes—and they opened them *really* early—until they finally shut them at what seemed like way too late at night, the twins were engaged in non-stop movement.

Six months ago, at the beginning of this whole exhausting adventure, Brady had thought that someone from either Gord's family or Gina's would challenge him for custody of the twins. But it turned out that long before her demise, Gina had become estranged from her family. And while Gord's parents did care about their twin grandsons, they were an older couple, which was why they ultimately had to pass when it came to assuming custody of the boys. Gord's mother and father just didn't have the stamina or the energy to keep up with preschoolers who, Brady had no doubt, were first cousins to that cartoon Road Runner that dashed from one place to another, sometimes in midair.

Brady couldn't really blame Gord's parents. If he could have somehow, in good conscience, found a way to get out of this unexpected guardianship that had been thrust upon him, he definitely would have.

But with no one left to take in the twins—they would have had to go into foster care, which

Brady couldn't allow—he felt that he owed it to his friend to honor his wishes and keep the boys. Owed it to Gord even though the selfless act might very well ultimately wind up being the death of him.

He could swear that his hair was turning gray even though he was only twenty-nine.

If he had to make some sort of a comparison between what he was going through and life in general, he'd have to say that it was like walking into the middle of a war without a weapon *or* a handbook. Quite honestly, Brady felt that he didn't have a single clue as to what the rules were when it came to child rearing.

He didn't even know which side he was actually supposed to be on.

Did he side with the kids or did he take a stand? Or was it a little bit of both and if so, how would he know how little and how much?

He felt totally lost, not to mention outnumbered.

Until he had begun to spend more time with Toby and Tyler on a regular, far more personal level, Brady had actually believed that most children under the age of seven or eight were innocent and pretty much just mischievous.

As it turned out, he was the clueless one.

It took Brady a while, but he finally realized that he was dealing with two adorable, devious little con artists who were out to get away with as much as they possibly could at any given time.

He was ashamed to acknowledge it now, but because Toby and Tyler had such innocent-looking little faces, they actually had him believing that their parents allowed them to stay up late *every single night*. Not only that, but they claimed—"innocently" again—that they were allowed to eat whatever they wanted to whenever they wanted.

What they *didn't* want to eat were vegetables or anything that could be viewed as even remotely healthy. Because he had grown up with Gord, who had been just as carefree, wild and unpredictable as his twin sons were now, Brady believed all these wild allegation that the twins were solemnly telling him—at first.

But then it slowly began to dawn on him that even Gord would have put his foot down at some point. And even if his friend hadn't, Brady became convinced that his friend's wife, Gina, would have.

It was around that time of his awakening that Brady realized that he couldn't allow things to glide like this any longer. He needed to do something about the situation—and fast—because it was all coming apart at the seams right before his very eyes.

The beginning of the end happened when his

exceedingly patient mother, Catherine, cornered him when he came home from work one night, admittedly late, from the sporting goods store that he managed.

He knew something was up by the expression on his mother's face before he even had a chance to close the door behind him.

"Come here, Brady," his mother called to him, patting the seat next to her on the sofa.

Tired from his long day, he crossed to Catherine on leaden feet as an urgent voice in his system cried *May-day*!

"You know I love you, don't you, Brady?" Catherine Fortune asked her son.

Brady's heart continued sinking. Opening statements like that didn't bode well. They only went downhill from there. Still, he tried to console himself, this was his mother he was dealing with.

He hoped for the best.

"Y-e-s?" Brady responded, drawing out the word as if doing that could somehow squash any negative message prefaced by that kind of opening statement.

Brady mentally crossed his fingers.

"And I wouldn't hurt you for the world," the tall, still-quite-handsome woman continued.

He could feel his heart sinking down even further in his chest.

"Go on," Brady said, bracing himself for the worst while desperately praying for the best—or at least not so "worst" if that was at all possible.

"But I quit," Catherine declared, informing her son with finality.

At first, the word—one he had never associated with his mother before now—wouldn't process.

"Quit?" he asked.

"Yes, quit," Catherine repeated, emphatically. "I can't babysit these little—heaven forgive me—*hellions* any longer."

His mother had never resorted to name calling or damning labels before. This had to be *really* bad.

"What happened, Mom?" Brady asked with a soul-weary sigh.

"They just won't listen to me," his mother complained. The whole situation was obviously a source of great pain for her. She didn't like leaving her son in a lurch like this, but the twins were just too much for her to handle. "And frankly, I'm getting too old for this."

"You're not old, Mom," Brady protested.

Catherine immediately cut him short before he could get any further. "Flattery isn't going to get you anywhere, darling."

Brady's mouth felt dry as he cast about for

some sort of a solution that would convince his mother to continue helping out with the twins.

"How about if I try to get them to promise that they'll behave?" he asked.

It was a desperate question asked by a desperate man because he hadn't a clue how to begin to get either of the twins to behave. If he had, he wouldn't have needed the help he was asking for.

Catherine pinned him with a look and summed up the situation neatly. "The only way you could get them to even remotely do that is by nailing the door to their room permanently shut. No, Brady, I'm sorry. It pains me greatly to say this, but my mind is made up." Rising, Catherine cupped her son's cheek with sorrowful affection. "I really hate to do this, darling, but I have no choice. Those boys have worn out my soul and you and I know that it's not going to get any better."

Brady felt as if his back was up against the proverbial wall and he had nowhere to turn. "What am I supposed to do, Mom?"

"Have you thought of sending them to military school?" Catherine Fortune suggested to her son in all seriousness.

"They're four, Mom," Brady pointed out. Because they were such whirlwinds of activity, it was a fact that had a habit of getting lost. "I don't think a military school would accept them. Be-

sides, I don't really want their spirits broken—
just contained. A lot," he added with feeling.

Catherine laughed softly under her breath as
she shook her head. "Well, good luck with that,"
she told Brady.

He was going to need more than luck, Brady
thought as he watched his mother leave.

For a time, after his mother had withdrawn
from her baby-sitting duties, he went through a
small army of nannies. Vetted by an agency, they
came—and went—with a fair amount of regu-
larity. Some of the nannies lasted for a couple of
weeks, others lasted only for a couple of days.

But they all had one thing in common. None
of them lasted for long. Some left cryptic comments in their wake, others left in icy, stony silence.

Like the other nannies who had left before
her, the short, squat woman looked like the very
epitome of the perfect nanny, but even Mildred
McGinty felt as if she was outmatched.

"I've been a professional nanny for twenty-
seven years, Mr. Fortune, and I have never,
never encountered such insufferable, rude, dis-
respectful children in all that time." Mrs. Mc-
Ginty drew herself up to appear taller than her
actual 5'1" height. "I believed I could put up with
anything, but today was the absolute *last* straw.

I caught those two demons—" she pointed a trembling finger in the general direction of the twins "—trying to toast marshmallows *in the middle of the living room floor*! Somehow, they found matches. If I hadn't been there, your whole house could have burned down—and most likely would have!" she declared angrily just before she slammed the front door behind her, permanently storming out of Brady's house.

Well, that would explain the soot marks, Brady thought wearily, looking down at the telltale marks in the middle of the throw rug.

Tyler was pulling on the edge of Brady's jacket. "We're sorry, Unca Brady," the twin said, looking contrite—at least for the moment.

"Yeah, we didn't mean to set the rug on fire," Toby piped up. Of the two overactive dynamos, Toby was the unofficial ringleader. "It just got in the way."

At least they knew enough to apologize, Brady thought. He knew he was grasping at straws, but straws, or pieces of them, were all he had.

They weren't malicious kids, he told himself, just really, really mischievous. Somehow, some way, that mischief needed to be tamed and contained, Brady decided in desperation.

But how?

He had been through an army of nannies, as well as sitters, and that clearly wasn't working.

Damn, but he needed help, Brady thought wearily. Big-time.

And soon.

And then suddenly, as if in a prophesy-like vision, he thought of Rambling Rose, the small Texas town he'd taken the twins to in January. At the time it was for his nephew's first birthday celebration. His older brothers Adam and Kane had resettled there, and they couldn't stop talking about how great the place was. They kept stressing how very family-oriented the town was.

He had resisted buying into the idea of living there, although his brothers did their best to talk him into it. At the time he was happy living near their folks in Upstate New York, happy with his job and his lifestyle—but all that was quickly changing and truthfully, it wasn't even his lifestyle any longer. Abject chaos had replaced what had once been his carefree existence, wiping out weekends spent with friends, watching sports and playing cards, not to mention dating. Nothing serious, but something he had looked forward to. Now there was no time for any of that.

Now all he wanted, heaven help him, was some sort of peace and quiet—or at the very least the *promise* of peace and quiet. As a matter of fact, given everything that was currently going on, he had begun to feel that he was willing to sell his soul for that.

Funny how things had a way of changing, Brady thought. His requirements had been a great deal different six months ago.

All right, onward and upward, he told himself.

Brady wondered just how surprised his family would be if he suddenly turned up with the twins in tow in the middle of the night.

Chapter Two

A month later and life in Texas still hadn't gotten any easier, Brady thought, trying hard not to let it all get to him.

Knowing he had to do something, Brady had uprooted the twins as well as himself from what was swiftly shaping up to be a hopelessly chaotic life and brought them to Rambling Rose. He felt that making the move during winter break from preschool was the best time to make the change. That way, everyone would be in downtime and the twins would have a chance to meet and get to know some of the kids in the area.

There was only one problem with that. There was no "winter break" in Rambling Rose. That meant although he had promised the boys there would be kids for them to play with in this new town, at the moment, there weren't any around. All the kids in town were attending school.

"There's no one to play with, Unca Brady," Tyler lamented for what seemed like at least the tenth time that day.

"Yeah, you said there were gonna be kids to play with. But there aren't any," Toby said in what could only be construed as an indignant manner.

After being around the twins for these last six-plus months now, Brady had learned that this sort of whining could only get worse, not better. Not only that, but it was liable to continue for *hours*.

Brady looked around at all the towering boxes that were lined up in almost every room. He had planned to make at least a decent dent in unpacking them today and putting some of the things away.

But his sanity took precedent over neatness—and he was fighting to preserve the former.

Knowing that all the kids were in school, desperate, he made a spur-of-the-moment decision.

"Well, if the kids aren't going to come to you, you're going to go to the kids," Brady declared. He could tell by the looks on their faces that the twins had no idea what he was talking about. It didn't matter. He knew what he had to do.

"Okay, boys, get ready. As soon as I find what I need to take with me, we're leaving," he told Toby and Tyler, thinking of the papers he needed to properly register the twins in school.

In the scheme of things, this was far more important than finding the right cupboard to house the dishes or where to put the pots and pans.

But it seemed that the twins apparently needed some convincing.

"Where are we going, Unca Brady? Huh? Where?" Toby wanted to know, shifting from foot to foot as Brady plowed through several boxes, searching for the custody papers he knew the preschool would want.

The papers wound up being housed in a red folder at the bottom of the third box. He had deliberately placed the custody papers in a red folder to make locating them easier. The only problem was that he'd forgotten which box he had placed the folder in.

He supposed that he should be grateful that he hadn't left the box back in New York, he told himself.

"Where, where, where?" Toby continued to ask, reciting the single word over and over again like some sort of a mantra.

"Preschool," Brady answered. "I'm registering the two of you at preschool."

"But we already went to preschool," Tyler told

him. He drew himself up as if that was the end of the discussion. "We're done."

"Oh no, you're not. Not by a long shot," Brady told the boys. "This is a new preschool."

Toby tilted his head, studying his guardian. "Is it like the old one?" he wanted to know.

This could go either way, Brady thought, so mentally, he flipped a coin, took a chance and said, "Yes."

"Then we don't wanna go," Toby informed his beleaguered guardian.

Brady pressed his lips together to suppress a few choice words he knew he could no longer utter in the company of children. Venting, even though it might make him feel better, was no longer permitted.

"That's where the kids are," he told the twins. "Oh."

Momentarily stumped, Toby looked at his brother, then motioned for Tyler to follow him to the corner and confer over this newest development.

Reaching the private "conference" area, the twins lowered their voices, something that Brady wasn't used to, considering their usual pitch was much higher. Glancing in his direction, the twins conferred with one another about the situation.

Brady wanted to prod them along but something in his gut told him this was a necessary process to help cement the still-very-new tenuous relationship between the twins and him. So he waited.

Finally, Toby raised his head and both boys looked up at their guardian. "Okay," Toby declared. "We'll go to preschool."

"Good choice," Brady told them, silently adding, *It's also your only choice.*

He had no desire to strong-arm the twins, but he would if he had to. Toby and Tyler were definitely going to preschool whether they liked it or not. He preferred them liking it, but if worse came to worse, he knew what he had to do.

"So, boys, what do you think?" Brady asked the twins less than an hour later as they stood on the preschool grounds. He thought that this process might be made a little easier if the boys felt that they had some sort of say in the matter.

"It's big," Tyler finally said as he looked around, his eyes huge with wonder.

Brady picked up on the one twin's awe. He didn't want the boy to feel overwhelmed. "It won't look so big once you get used to it."

Toby looked as if he was ready to begin exploring right then and there. He yanked on Brady's hand. "Can we get used to it now, Unca Brady?" he wanted to know, pulling again, harder this time. "Can we, huh, can we?"

Brady tightened his grip on both boys' hands because he knew that Tyler would follow his twin's lead and would begin pulling him in a minute. They weren't strong, but their enthusiasm made them very difficult to manage.

"Not yet," Brady responded. "First we need to sign you up."

Toby's face puckered up as he tried to understand. "What's that?" he wanted to know.

"That's when they put your name on a sign," Tyler explained.

Uncertain, Toby turned toward Brady. "Is that what they do?"

"Close enough," Brady answered. He wasn't about to waste any more time standing outside the preschool. He wanted to get the boys *inside* the building.

Still holding onto each twin, he found himself grateful that Gord and Gina had only had twins and not triplets because he'd be out of hands.

Mindful over every step he had to take, Brady carefully guided the boys, who were behaving more like squirming puppies than flesh-and-blood children, into the school's registration office.

The moment he walked in, Brady became instantly aware of the short, dour-looking woman seated at the registration desk.

Harriet Ferguson, according to the nameplate

on her desk, continued watching him as made his way over to her as he held on to each of the twins.

"Ms. Ferguson?" he asked, knowing it was a needless question. The woman nodded. Taking a breath, Brady pushed on. "I'm Brady Fortune. I called earlier about registering Toby and Tyler here at your preschool." He nodded toward the twins.

There appeared to be no sign of any sort of recognition on the woman's part.

Instead, Ms. Ferguson shifted razor-sharp eyes to appraise the barely restrained twins. "I take it you don't put much store in disciplining these two." She pressed her lips together in disapproval. "I'm afraid that your sons might fare better someplace else—"

There wasn't so much as a touch of warmth in her voice, Brady realized. But he needed the boys to be accepted here. This was the only way he'd be able to work, to take care of all those errands that never seemed to end, to be sure he could provide all of the things the boys needed to grow up safe and healthy. And he really wanted the boys to make some friends their own age, too.

Having nothing to lose, Brady decided to plunge in.

"They're not my sons," he told the woman.

Ms. Ferguson looked a little taken aback by

that. "I don't understand." It was obvious that hadn't been discussed. "Then why—"

"I'm their guardian," he told her, anticipating the woman's question. "I'm afraid that their parents were rather lax when it came to discipline and instituting any sort of structure. Actually, until just recently," Brady confessed, "Toby and Tyler had never even been inside a nursery school, much less attended one. Boys, stop it," Brady cried, trying to get the twins to settle down until he could at least finish getting them registered.

"Humph, I can readily believe that," Ms. Ferguson said in a dismissive tone. "But as I started to say earlier—"

Anticipating getting torpedoed out of the water, Brady quickly interjected, "It's not just that these boys aren't used to having a structured day—I'm afraid that they're dealing with something far more serious." Seeing that he had caught the woman's attention, he pushed on. "Six months ago, they lost both their parents in a motorcycle accident. *That's* why I have custody of them.

"I'm not ashamed to say that this is all really new to me." He laughed almost self-deprecatingly. "Six months ago I was living in upstate New York, managing a sporting goods store and dealing with adults practically on an exclusive basis. Now—"

He raised his hands in a hapless fashion as he looked at the squirming boys.

"I'm clearly out of my depth here, but I am trying," he stressed. Brady looked at the woman, giving it his all as he exuded charm. "Will you help me, Ms. Ferguson? Will you register Toby and Tyler at your school so I can begin the process of getting these two boys to settle down a little?"

"It's *Mrs.* Ferguson," the woman pointedly corrected him. "And yes, I will register them—provided you have all the necessary paperwork with you, of course," she qualified.

Brady pulled out the red folder he had brought with him. "I have everything all right here," he assured the woman, placing the folder in front of Mrs. Ferguson on her desk.

With short, almost regal movement, Mrs. Ferguson opened the folder and glanced through the pages that were contained there. She raised her hazel eyes to look at him when she was done.

"Well, you're organized. That's a good first step," she told him.

Because Brady had brought everything he could possibly think of that might be even remotely be required, the process, mercifully, went rather quickly.

Finished inputting all the information into the

computer, Mrs. Ferguson rested her fingers on the keyboard and raised her eyes to look at his.

"All right, Mr. Fortune, I need one last thing from you." Her voice was almost pregnant with meaning.

At this point Brady felt exhilarated and almost giddy. He had actually managed to get the twins registered—well, almost registered—and he was willing to do anything to reach the finish line.

"What do you need?" he asked, then, still riding the wave of exhilaration, answered his own question. "A kidney? Because if you require a kidney, you've got it! Just name the hospital," he told her.

Mrs. Ferguson almost smiled, Brady observed. "That's very generous of you, Mr. Fortune, but no, a kidney won't be necessary. But I will need a list of people who are authorized to pick up your twins if you're not able to come."

That caught him off guard. He thought of his mother and the fact that she had thrown up her hands in the end. He didn't want to put any undue burdens on his family. But in the end, he knew he had to comply with Mrs. Ferguson's request, especially since, logically, if he was going to be working, he'd certainly need to ask his siblings for help.

So he gave her the names of his brothers, Adam and Kane, who were living here in Rambling Rose, and whose children were enrolled at the same school. Adam's one-year-old son, Larkin, was in the day care program, and Kane had recently gotten engaged to Layla McCarthy whose two-year-old daughter, Erin, was in one of the older groups. Kane couldn't wait to become Erin's official dad, although he had obviously already taken the little girl into his heart.

Maybe I should be asking Kane for parenting advice, Brady mused.

Tired of being patient, not to mention quiet, Toby spoke up. "I wanna go play now," he cried, tugging hard on Brady's hand. "Are you done yet? Huh? Are you?" the boy wanted to know, all but ready to jump out of his skin if he didn't do something soon.

This was nothing new, Brady thought. But what was new was what Tyler said just as Toby pulled free.

"I want to stay here with you," the other twin told him.

Tyler had caught him totally by surprise. Brady wasn't prepared for that.

Neither was he prepared to have the boy all but wrap himself around his leg, holding on for dear life as if he was hermetically sealed to it.

Brady put a comforting hand on the boy's head. "Hey, Ty, what's up?"

Tyler looked up at him wearing the most serious expression Brady could recall ever seeing on the twin's face.

"I don't wanna leave you," Tyler cried.

In an instant, Toby was on his twin's other side, tugging at his brother's arm. "Yeah, you do," he told Tyler. "We're here to play!" he declared as if it was a battle cry.

Torn, feeling suddenly helpless, Brady looked toward the unsmiling gatekeeper, silently asking Mrs. Ferguson for help.

Mrs. Ferguson appeared to visibly soften right before his eyes.

"The boys will be fine," she assured him. "But in my opinion, *you* could definitely use some help."

Uh-oh, here it came. He knew that look, Brady thought. Mrs. Ferguson was about to recommend either a psychiatrist or a psychologist to help sort out this messy situation. Either way, he wasn't interested. He didn't need therapy. He needed help managing the twins. He needed help with his kids.

His kids. God. Would he ever get used to those words?

Meanwhile Mrs. Ferguson was apparently searching for something in her desk drawer.

"Ah, here it is," she said triumphantly, holding up the business card she had just found and passing it to him. "There you go."

Nodding his head, Brady forced himself to smile as he took the card from her. He glanced at the name imprinted on it. It read H. Radcliffe and included a phone number on it.

Without comment, Brady shoved the card into his pocket. He had no intention of calling who-ever this was. In fact, he planned to toss it away the moment he left the building.

But for now, he played the game.

"Thank you," he said, nodding his head at the older woman.

"You're most welcome," Mrs. Ferguson responded. She gave him a penetrating look, as if she could read his thoughts. "I would call that number if I were you," she emphasized.

The next moment, the woman was on her phone, making a call.

Brady took that as his cue to leave, but when he started to, one hand around each twin's hand, Mrs. Ferguson held up her forefinger, keeping the harried guardian in his place.

"Jenny?" she said to whoever picked up the phone on the other end, "I have two new students who need to be brought to Mrs. Nelson's room."

"Who's Mrs. Nelson?" Toby wanted to know, not bothering to keep his voice down.

"I don't want to go to her room," Tyler cried, once again wrapping himself around Brady's leg.

Mrs. Ferguson had no sooner hung up than

the young woman she had called—Jenny, looking as if she had been one of the students here a short while ago—stepped inside the registration office.

"You called, Mrs. Ferguson?" the lively-looking young blonde asked.

"Yes, I did." The administrator gestured toward the twins. "Toby and Tyler need to be taken to their new classroom," she told Jenny, then turned toward Brady. "You're free to go now, Mr. Fortune. Don't forget to get a more complete list back to me," she reminded him.

Brady watched as the twins left with the young woman who was escorting them to their new classroom. Tyler looked back at him and waved tearfully. Nervous for the first time about leaving them, Brady waved back.

"Don't worry," Mrs. Ferguson told him, noting the concerned look on his face. "I promise that they will be fine. And you should call that number," Mrs. Ferguson reminded Brady. There was a finality in her voice that all but sent him on his way.

"Yeah, right," Brady murmured, watching until Toby and Tyler disappeared from his line of sight.

Time for him to go, too, he thought. He realized he still hadn't eaten anything, even though he'd made breakfast for the twins before taking them to school. Maybe he would stop at the Hotel Fortune for that breakfast and some really strong coffee, emphasis on the latter.

The sooner, the better, he thought.

The thought sustained Brady as he drove away from the preschool.

He forgot all about the business card in his pocket.

Chapter Three

"Hi, Cowboy. What brings you by to my neck of the woods?"

The question, asked in a melodious voice, had Brady abandoning his thoughts and looking up to see his cousin Nicole Fortune. The executive chef of Roja was standing beside his small table holding a pot of coffee in her hand. There was a wide, welcoming smile on her lips.

"So, can I interest you in another cup of coffee since you seemed to have drained that one?" she asked, nodding at the empty cup sitting right in front of him.

"You twisted my arm," Brady told her, then

asked, "Would it look bad if I just drank that coffee straight out of the pot?"

Nicole laughed as she poured her cousin a second cup. Then, setting the pot down on the table, she slid into the booth opposite Brady. "That bad, huh?" she asked sympathetically.

Brady took an extra-long gulp of the inky black coffee, letting it wind all through him before he put the cup down and addressed her question.

"You have no idea," he replied with a sigh.

"You're right, I probably don't," Nicole readily admitted. "Talk to me, cousin," she urged. "That's what I'm here for."

Brady smiled at her. "Not that I don't appreciate the offer, Nicole, but don't you have enough work to do?" He glanced around the restaurant. "I mean, it can't be easy, running the kitchen and keeping everything flowing smoothly."

"You're absolutely right, it's not," Nicole agreed. "But I've got good people working for me and right now, the morning rush is over and the afternoon insanity hasn't started yet, so I'm free for a few minutes." She leaned forward over the table for two, putting her hand over his, silently urging her cousin to open up to her.

"C'mon, Brady. Two ears, no waiting. Talk," she coaxed. When he didn't begin to bare his soul to her, she made her best guess at what was bothering Brady. "Is the move getting you down? I know that Rambling Rose has to be a huge change from New York for you, but—"

"Oh, it is," Brady assured her. "But it's actually a nice change." He thought how accommodating all of his cousins had been from the moment he had let them know he was coming to Texas with the twins. Busy though they were, they had even taken the time to help him find a cozy three-bedroom home in a very reasonable price range. He couldn't have asked for anything more. "I know I could definitely get used to the peace and quiet—if I could find some peace and quiet," he qualified wistfully with another sigh.

Nicole arched a well-shaped eyebrow, slightly confused by Brady's comment. "You're going to have to explain that," she told him. "My brain is currently in slow gear."

"Fair enough." He readily admitted that his previous statement might have sounded cryptic and confusing. "Let me put it another way. Six months ago my biggest decision was which bar to hit on a Saturday night. Now I'm constantly putting out small fires—" he thought of the aborted marshmallow roast the twins had once planned to hold on the living room floor back in New York "—sometimes literally." His laugh was self-deprecating. It helped him cope. "I tell you, I have newfound respect for my parents. Those two people managed to raise eight kids—two of whom were twins—without losing their minds. Looking back now, I realize that had to be one hell of a juggling act on their part." He shook his head. "Honestly, I'm surprised that they didn't both drink themselves into a stupor every night."

Nicole smiled knowingly, having gleaned the one significant kernel out of her cousin's rambling narrative. "So we're talking about the twins."

Brady nodded vigorously. "Oh yes, we're definitely talking about the twins," he confirmed. "Do you know that with all her experience and all her knowledge, my mother actually threw in the towel after trying to look after Toby and Tyler? That woman raised *six* active kids and yet those two four-year-olds turned out to be too much for her."

Her cousin looked really worn out, Nicole thought. If anyone was ever sorely in need of a pep talk, it was Brady.

"You're overlooking one important thing, Brady," she told him.

"And that's what?" he asked. "That Toby and Tyler are really space aliens?"

"No, silly," Nicole laughed. "When Aunt Catherine was 'effortlessly' raising all of you little critters, she was younger than she is now.

A *lot* younger," his cousin emphasized. "And age makes a huge difference, trust me." She smiled at Brady encouragingly as she watched him consume more coffee. "Give Rambling Rose a little time to work its magic on those kids. They'll settle down a bit before you know it. Probably not a whole lot, mind you, but enough for you to survive the exhausting process of raising them.

"Right now, from what I hear," Nicole continued, feeling that he needed a bit more support, "you're holding your own and doing a damn fine job—especially for a 'clueless bachelor,'" she told him with another wide, encouraging smile.

"I *do* think I've done a damned good job," Brady agreed with his cousin, "considering the situation and my total lack of experience."

Nicole's eyes crinkled with humor. "Well, I see that your ego hasn't been damaged any in the process."

Rather than laughing, a dubious look came over Brady's face. He was taking this conversation seriously, she realized.

"Well, by all rights it should have been," he told Nicole.

Her brow furrowed. "Again, you're going to have to explain that, Brady. I'm afraid I don't follow you."

His thoughts were coming into his head in daunting snippets. He really did need to get hold of himself before someone decided he actually *did* need a shrink.

"I just registered the twins for preschool today," Brady told his cousin.

The fact that Brady was here at Roja by himself had just hit her. "I should have asked you where you managed to stash those little wild mustangs."

"They're at the preschool where I registered them." He felt he was repeating himself, but then, maybe he hadn't been all that clear earlier. But then, he was still frustrated at Mrs. Ferguson's less-than-veiled suggestion that he get psychiatric help.

Incensed all over again, Brady said, "Do you know what that woman who runs the school had the gall to imply?" He didn't wait for Nicole to ask him "What?" but went straight to the answer. "That I needed a shrink. She doesn't even know me. Where does she get off saying that to me?"

"Maybe from years of running the nursery school?" Nicole suggested, doing her best to keep the smile out of her voice. It wasn't funny, but his anger made him look adorable.

However, Brady wasn't buying the excuse Nicole made for Mrs. Ferguson. He dismissed the very thought.

"Well, I don't need therapy or someone telling me that all my problems stem from episodes of traumatic toilet training."

"Well, maybe not all your problems…" Nicole said, an amused smile playing on her lips.

"Very funny," Brady said. He knew he was overreacting and told himself to calm down. "If you didn't brew the best damn coffee I've ever had," he informed his cousin, "I'd take my business elsewhere."

"What business?" Nicole asked her cousin drolly. "Were you planning on paying for the breakfast you just had?"

Brady was about to answer that he hadn't come here to mooch off a member of his family when the words froze on his tongue, immobilized there by the sight of what had to be one of the most beautiful women he had ever seen. She had just walked into the restaurant, clutching a single sheet of paper in her hand.

Gorgeous though she was, the expression on her face made him think of a frightened deer that had wandered out of the forest and was desperately looking for a way back before she ran into a hunter.

Nicole's back was to the restaurant's doorway, but she saw the expression on her cousin's face. "What are you looking at, Brady?" She turned around to look in the same direction that her cousin was gazing in. Able to spot a job applicant a mile away, Nicole was instantly alert. "Uh-oh, unless I miss my guess, duty calls," she told Brady, then explained, "I put out the word that we were hiring.

"If you'll excuse me for a few minutes, this shouldn't take long," she predicted.

Nicole rose and made her way over to the woman, flashing a smile as she went.

When the young woman noticed her approaching, in Nicole's opinion she looked both relieved and apprehensive at the same time.

Very mysterious, Nicole thought.

Reaching the other woman, Nicole put out her hand. "Hi, I'm Nicole Fortune, executive chef of Roja," she said by way of an introduction. "May I be of some service?"

In response, the young woman nervously all but thrust the paper she was holding into Nicole's outstretched hand. "Hello." The woman said the word almost as if it was an afterthought. "Um, I heard that Roja might be looking for help and well—" she flushed a little "—I'm looking for a job."

Nicole looked down at the paper and realized that it was a résumé. However, it wasn't exactly in keeping with the kind of resume she was looking for.

While Nicole focused on the menu, she had made certain that she was familiar with all the various aspects of running a restaurant, from the kitchen staff to the waitstaff. Though hiring the latter was usually the job of the general manager, she was filling in today.

Judging by the résumé the applicant had just given her, none of these things were even remotely familiar to the woman who was standing before her.

Nicole raised her eyes to look at the young woman. "I don't see any references on here to you having any cooking or experience waiting tables," Nicole pointed out.

"That's because I don't have any—but I'm a quick study," the woman added in a hasty postscript.

Nicole looked the woman over with a discerning eye. Though she was well-dressed, the petite woman with the long brown hair and warm chocolate-brown eyes seemed to have a slightly desperate air about her.

This wasn't going to work out, Nicole thought. She tried to let the hopeful applicant down gently. "While it is true that we are looking to hire a few people, the hotel, and so by extension, the restaurant, is only looking to hire locals at the moment."

"Oh, but I am a local," the young woman assured Nicole quickly. Then, in the interest of honesty, she corrected herself. "That is, I've been living in Rambling Rose for the last three months. But that counts, doesn't it?" she asked hopefully.

The chef frowned a little. "I'm not sure if that actually qualifies." In response to the disappointment she saw on the young woman's face, Nicole had a slight change of heart. "Tell you what, I'll talk to our hotel manager and then I'll get back to you," she promised. "As soon as possible." Nicole smiled kindly, then excused herself and headed back into the kitchen

The lightly tanned young woman's cheeks turned a shade of pink. She knew when she was being dismissed. Mustering what dignity she could, she murmured, "Well, thank you for your time," as she turned away.

From his vantage point at the table, Brady had been privy to this little minidrama and he found himself utterly intrigued by the woman applying for a job. Having just been in the same position himself recently, looking for work, he could totally sympathize with what she had to be going through. He, of course, had family to turn to and for that he was eternally grateful. Every single one of them had been warm and welcoming. Without their warm welcome and their help, settling in with the twins would have been so much more challenging.

For some reason, he got the feeling that this woman didn't have someone to turn to.

What was her story, he couldn't help wondering.

From the way she moved, not to mention the way she was dressed, Brady had already been able to tell that she wasn't someone who was accustomed to waitressing. There was just something about her body language, the way she carried herself, that told him she wasn't the type who balanced plates on a tray for a living.

So why was she here, looking to apply for a job as a waitress? Could she be down on her luck? He could feel another wave of sympathy swelling up within him.

Half rising in the booth, Brady attempted to get the woman's attention.

"Excuse me," he began, watching her face for a response. When she shifted her brown eyes to look in his direction, he saw that she looked a little leery. "I couldn't help overhearing," he began, then realized that might not be the best approach. He tried again. "Look, can I buy you a cup of coffee? Maybe you'd like to talk," he suggested. He nodded at the empty seat facing his.

She looked somewhat apprehensively at the stranger. While he did sound sympathetic, she knew she couldn't just open up to him. For one thing, she didn't know this man from Adam—

and she was well-aware of how misconstrued things could be.

The young woman gathered her shoulder bag to her. "Look, I really should be going," she told him. With that, she began to put space between them and headed toward the exit.

Maybe she misunderstood his offer, Brady thought. Raising his voice, he told her, "I wasn't trying to hit on you," before she had a chance to open the door. "I've got my hands filled with my kids."

The woman stopped then and slowly, almost reluctantly, turned around to face him.

Brady took it as a good sign. But he remained where he was, using the sound of his voice to draw her back. "I was just looking for someone to talk to, nothing else, I promise," he told her, raising his hands as a sign of innocence.

There was something about the stranger's voice that broke through the barriers that she had newly erected around herself. And, even though she told herself this could all be just a lie to draw her in, the young woman scrutinized the friendly stranger for a long moment.

"What is it that you want to talk about?" she finally asked him.

Brady nodded toward his table. "Then you'll have coffee with me?"

She pressed her lips together, debating accepting the invitation.

"Well, I guess that I could use the coffee..." she began rather hesitantly.

"Great," Brady enthused. "Then I won't feel so bad about bending your ear," he said with a warm laugh that seemed to corkscrew right into her chest.

Looking around the restaurant, Brady raised his hand and managed to catch the eye of the lone waitress who was on duty at the moment.

Seeing him, the waitress came over to their table. "What can I get you?" she asked, looking from one occupant to the other.

"Could you bring a cup of coffee for the lady?" Brady requested.

The waitress nodded. "Sure thing," she responded obligingly. And then she promised to "be right back," as she quickly left to get the coffee.

"Okay, now that that's taken care of, take a seat," Brady said, then added, "Please," when the woman still looked as if she was undecided about staying.

Brady noticed that when the stranger did sit down, she perched on the edge of the seat, like someone who was prepared to make a quick getaway if it came down to that.

Again, he couldn't help wondering just what

this person's story was. A woman who looked the way she did shouldn't have a care in the world, but it was apparent that she did.

Big-time if he didn't miss his guess.

Maybe he could draw her out if he told her a little about himself, Brady thought just as the waitress returned with the coffee.

"Will there be anything else?" the waitress asked, looking from Brady to his new coffee companion.

Brady, in turn, looked at the woman sitting opposite him, raising an eyebrow as he asked her, "Would you like anything else? Maybe a croissant?" he suggested.

But the young woman shook her head. "No, thank you. The coffee will do just fine. Really," she stressed.

The waitress nodded. "Well, if you change your minds, just let me know," she told them cheerfully. "My shift doesn't end for another couple of hours," she added just before she withdrew, leaving the two of them alone to share whatever stories they had to tell.

The woman was barely out of sight before the awkwardness set in and for the moment, all conversation faded.

Chapter Four

Harper had to admit that she felt just a little awkward sitting here like this opposite a complete stranger.

"So tell me about these kids who you said were filling your hands," Harper, the woman sitting opposite Brady, said after taking a sip of her coffee.

"Toby and Tyler," Brady said, giving his coffee companion their names. "They're twins," he added as if that should explain everything, including why he was so frazzled. "I just finished registering them at the preschool." The experience vividly brought back the feelings of resentment that had been raised. "Do you know what the woman at the registration office had the nerve to imply?" He didn't wait to be asked to elaborate. Instead, Brady told her, "That I needed a psychologist."

Though she was trying to be sympathetic, Harper didn't see the problem. Was she missing something? "Why would that annoy you so much?" she asked, reading between the lines and interpreting his reaction to what she viewed as a well-meaning suggestion. "Everyone needs a little help sometimes." She could see by the look in his eyes that the man was distancing himself from both her and her suggestion. Harper decided to attempt another approach. "If you don't mind my asking, where's the twins' mother?"

Brady drew himself up, his body language telling her that she had just crossed a line and to back off. "She's dead," he answered.

Harper had no idea the man was a widower. And at such a young age. Her heart instantly went out to him. "Oh, I am so sorry," she told him, not wanting to scratch what could possibly be a fresh wound. "Maybe the three of you—you and your boys—could benefit from some counseling. This has to be a very difficult time for all of you," she told him compassionately.

As she watched, the stranger's face clouded over.

"It is extremely hard," Brady informed her

coldly. This was a mistake, he thought. "And having a total stranger sitting in judgment over my actions doesn't help."

Did he mean her? Just in case he did, Harper backed away from the topic. "I'm sorry—I didn't mean to offend you," she began.

But Brady was already on his feet. "No," he told her. "The fault is mine. I was the one who engaged you in conversation when I shouldn't have." His tone left no room for any further exchange. His nerves felt raw.

Taking out a twenty, he left it on the table between her cup of coffee and his. "That should cover everything. Have a nice day," he told the woman crisply.

And then he walked away.

That settled it, Harper thought, getting up from the table herself. All men were crazy.

At least he had done something positive, Brady thought, attempting to comfort himself when he went to pick up the twins a few hours later. If nothing else, he had managed to get the boys registered for preschool. One thing down, four million to go.

After parking his car in the school lot, he was unsure just where to go to pick up the boys. Deciding to take a chance, he followed the gaggle of parents who gathered at one of the gate entrances on the far side of the schoolyard.

He kept his eyes peeled, afraid he might miss connecting with the twins. But he needn't have worried. When the preschoolers and kindergarteners came pouring out of the building, he spotted his two immediately.

And then his heart sank.

Tyler was crying. The boy made a beeline for him the instant Tyler saw him.

Toby was a couple of steps behind his brother and the moment he saw the boy, Brady could tell that Tyler's twin had been in a fight.

Tyler threw his arms around him while Toby, looking guilty, hung back.

"Okay," Brady began, bracing himself. "What happened?"

The question was for both of the twins, but only Tyler answered him. His voice trembled and it was obvious that he was either on the verge of tears, or had just *stopped* crying.

"I didn't think you were coming back, Unca Brady. I was so scared," he added after a beat.

That really got to him. Brady put his arm around the boys, hugging them both. "You know I'd never leave you, boys. I brought you here so you could play with the other kids. You were supposed to have fun," he reminded the twins, "not worry about me coming back—because I'll always come back for you," he assured Tyler. "For both of you," he stressed, looking over at Toby. "Okay, what's your story?" he asked the other twin.

Toby turned to him, then looking a little too innocent, and replied, "No story."

Brady raised a skeptical eyebrow. "Then why do you look like you were in a fight?" he wanted to know.

It was Tyler who piped up with an answer. "'Cause he was in a fight."

"Toby, is this true?" Brady asked the disheveled twin, placing his hand on the boy's shoulders.

Toby shrugged his small shoulders and looked off into the distance. "Maybe," he finally admitted.

"Okay, and why were you fighting?" Brady wanted to know.

Tyler shrugged again, but this time he followed the action up with an answer. "'Cause that kid made fun of Tyler." Toby vaguely pointed off into the distance. There were still a number of children in that area. "He called Tyler a baby for crying. I made him take it back," he added proudly.

"Look, Toby," Brady told the twin wearily, "while I think it's great that you stood up for your brother, you can't settle things by pummeling people who annoy you."

Toby's brow furrowed. "What's pum-pum— that word?" he finally asked.

"It means beating up the other guy," Brady explained to Toby, then stressed, "You can't do that."

"How come?" Toby asked, confused. And then he proudly declared, "I won."

"Because eventually, someone might wind up beating *you* up when you come out swinging and I'd rather that didn't happen." Feeling as if his lecture was going nowhere, Brady decided it was time to wind it up. "C'mon, guys, let's go home."

Taking each twin by the hand, Brady brought them to his vehicle.

After securing the twins into their separate car seats in the rear, Brady set out for home.

Maybe that woman in the registration office, Mrs. Ferguson, was right, he thought as he drove. Maybe he did need help.

One thing was for sure—this certainly wasn't going the way he had hoped it would. If it was, by now his own life should have been settling down into some kind of orderly routine. Instead, it felt as if the chaos was only growing, absorbing him.

If it got any worse, he was fairly certain that it would wind up swallowing him up whole.

Trying to smother the desperate feeling he felt bubbling up inside him, Brady thought of the card that Mrs. Ferguson had given him. He hadn't had time to throw it away yet, the way he had planned.

Slipping his hand into his pocket to make sure it was still there, he came in contact with the business card. Okay, that settled it.

He decided to make the call.

What harm would it do? And who knew, maybe talking to this H. Radcliffe guy might even help him. It certainly couldn't make it any worse.

He realized that Toby was asking him a question. "We going back tomorrow?"

"Yes," Brady answered, bracing himself for a fight. "You are."

Toby totally surprised him by saying "Cool."

It was Tyler, the more quiet of the pair, who protested, "I don't wanna go!"

"It'll get better," Brady promised automatically. "Besides, you don't want to be known as a quitter, do you?" he asked, thinking that would convince the twin to go back.

But again, Brady discovered he was wrong.

"Why not?" Toby challenged him.

Everything was always a debate, Brady thought wearily. "Just give it another shot, okay?" he asked, then added, "For me," for good measure.

But it was Toby who shocked him by telling his twin, "I'll be there to take care of you, Ty."

Brady looked up in the rearview mirror to see Tyler's reaction. The boy still looked somewhat unconvinced, but he didn't protest any further.

When they got home, Brady made sandwiches for the boys and put out two servings of grapes as dessert. While the twins were busy eating—and using the grapes to lob at each other—Brady went to place a call to H. Radcliffe.

He was more than ready to admit that he needed help—but instead he found himself leaving a voice mail.

According to the message, H. Radcliffe was out of the office.

Most likely saving someone else's sanity, Brady thought. The next moment, he found himself talking quickly in hopes that H. Radcliffe would get back to him sometime today. Right now, it was the only thing Brady had to cling to.

"Hello, this is Brady Fortune. You don't know me, but Mrs. Ferguson at the Rambling Rose preschool suggested I get in contact with you. She's the one who gave me your card," he added, thinking that might help tip the scale in his favor. "I've recently become the guardian for four-year-old twins and I realize that I'm *really* out of my depth here. I could really use any help I can get. Please give me a call back as soon as possible. I'll be waiting for your call," he added for good measure. And then he left his number.

Brady was aware that the polite way to go would have been to say *at your earliest convenience*, but at this point, he felt the situation was way beyond anyone's convenience. Certainly beyond his. His life felt as if it was in a state of constant emergency and he desperately needed help dealing with it *now*.

Brady ended the call just as he heard a crash coming from the other room.

Brady went to investigate this latest threat to his peace and quiet, fervently hoping that H. Radcliffe would listen to his messages before going to bed tonight and give him a call.

Harper saw the blinking light on the landline in her studio apartment the moment she walked in. Crossing her fingers and hoping that this was about a possible job, she didn't even bother taking her jacket off. Instead, she went straight to the phone on the nightstand and hit the green arrow marked Play.

She listened to the message twice.

There was no doubt about it. Someone was calling about a possible position.

Someone wanted to hire her, Harper thought,

her heart leaping up in her chest. Finally, just when she had begun to give up all hope, there was suddenly a light at the end of this extremely long, dark tunnel.

What that meant, she thought, was that she didn't have to convince that chef at Roja that she had what it took to be a waitress—because truthfully, she really didn't.

Now, with any luck, she could actually get back to what she was good at—being a nanny.

Harper played the message for a third time to make sure she wasn't getting ahead of herself.

No, she wasn't wrong, she thought. The man who had placed the call definitely sounded as if he was looking for a nanny, no doubt about it.

It also occurred to her that the voice on the phone sounded somewhat familiar, but even though she concentrated, she couldn't place the voice.

Maybe, she decided, it was her imagination.

It didn't matter, though. All that mattered was getting back to what she loved doing —working with children. If she got this job, that could wind up being the answer to all her problems. She didn't even care about the salary.

Harper smiled to herself.

Just when she was ready to give up, the sun had broken through the clouds. Apparently moving to Rambling Rose hadn't been the beginning of the end for her. It had wound up being only an excruciatingly long, but ultimately temporary pause.

In truth, she had never wanted to come out here in the first place. A few months ago, she had been working in Dallas as a nanny. But when Justine Wheeler, the woman she had been working for, had been transferred to Rambling Rose by her employer, she had begged Harper to come with the family.

Harper had really wanted to say no, but she had trouble asserting herself, so she had agreed to the woman's pleas and wound up moving here even though her common sense told her not to.

It wasn't actually the location she had a problem with, it was the fact that the woman's husband had slowly become progressively more and more flirtatious.

She did her best to keep the man, Edward, at a distance, but apparently Justine's husband didn't accept any of her rebuffs as genuine. The situation between Harper and Edward had been a very touchy one at that point and the move to Rambling Rose only seemed to make things worse.

Harper loved the children she was taking care of, but more and more she found herself trying to politely avoid the woman's husband. While Edward Wheeler had always been nice to her, after they had made the move, he became a little *too* nice.

He grew even more flirtatious, a lot more than she was comfortable with.

When he made an outright, undeniable pass at her, Harper decided that she had no choice but to quit. But when she told Justine she was leaving, without citing the reason *why*, Justine once again begged her to remain, playing on her sympathies and her love for the children.

The woman did everything in her power to make her stay. She said that they were new in town, lamenting that they would never be able to replace her on such short notice.

So once again against her better judgment, Harper agreed to stay on. But, predictably, things only got worse. The Wheelers' marriage was coming apart at the seams. So when Justine saw her husband flirting with Harper, she got the totally wrong idea. She viciously blamed Harper for all her marital woes and fired her on the spot. She never gave her a chance to defend herself.

Harper had never once mentioned to Justine the uncomfortable situation she had endured all this time. At that point she knew that whatever she said wouldn't be believed anyway.

With that in mind, Harper packed up and left immediately.

Her only regret about leaving was the couple's

two little girls. The girls were heartbroken and cried when she left.

That was how she had wound up being jobless in a town where she didn't know anyone. She had no funds and with her parents gone, she had no one to go back to. Her only family was a brother who was currently in the army overseas. She was not about to ask him for any help. She had always taken pride in earning her own way. They did correspond, but not all that often. She refused to be the one in their relationship who just complained and unloaded, especially given the pressures he was under. So she kept her emails short and upbeat.

However, to make matters worse, Justine Wheeler had quickly begun spreading vicious lies about her so all of her potential nanny jobs quickly dried up. If she had any doubts that was happening, having the phone go dead in her ear quickly convinced her that this was true.

No one called the number on the cards that she had made up.

With her back against the wall and very little money in her pocket, Harper had started looking for any sort of work at all. That was how she had wound up interviewing for a waitressing job.

Quickly exhausting her meager savings, she needed money and she needed it fast.

Truthfully, she had given up all hope of get-

ting any sort of a position as a nanny. But someone had obviously decided to give her a try and
they had called the number on one of the numer-
ous cards that she had left scattered about the
town in her wake.

Harper's hand was trembling as she called
the number that was left on her voice mail. As
she listened to the phone on the other end ring,
she prayed that the person who had called was
home—and that he hadn't found a nanny yet.

Mentally, she counted off the number of rings.

Her heart had started to sink when the phone
rang six times.

The person wasn't home.

And then she heard the receiver being picked up.

She could feel her pulse going into overdrive.
Her mouth was dry, but even so, she forced herself to start talking.

Quickly.

Chapter Five

Harper had no idea why she felt so nervous. After all, it wasn't as if she was new to this whole thing. She had been a nanny for a number of years now. That meant that she had placed calls and made appointments for interviews before.

The problem right now was that she felt at the end of her rope and this could very well be the lifeline she had been hoping for—if she didn't somehow wind up messing everything up.

The deep voice echoed in her ear as she heard the man say, "Hello?"

Her heart lodged itself in her throat.

Here goes everything, Harper thought.

"Hello, Mr. Fortune? This is Harper Radcliffe.

You called me earlier today about needing my services," she said, trying to sound as cheerful as she could. She waited for his response. When there wasn't one immediately, Harper thought that his cell reception might have possibly gone down. "Hello, Mr. Fortune? Are you still there? Did you hear me?"

Brady had heard her—and there was something strangely familiar in her voice, but he couldn't quite figure out what it was. He shook his head and dismissed the sensation.

Realizing that the woman was still waiting for some sort of response, he answered, "Sorry. Yes, I heard you. Um, about the reason that I called," he began.

"Yes, of course." *Push on, Harper, push on*, she silently ordered. "Why don't I meet you at Provisions tomorrow, say about eleven o'clock, to discuss the matter? If that fits in with your schedule, of course," she quickly tacked on.

"Provisions," Brady repeated. Was that how these shrinks did things? Get you eating and then get you talking? Curious, he couldn't help asking, "Isn't that a little unusual?"

If this potential client had turned out to be a woman, she would have readily gone to their house. Harper thought. But this was a man and after her last experience with her employer's husband, she wanted to meet this man somewhere out in the open.

But she couldn't very well tell him that because he might take offense, so she said, "I prefer our first meeting to take place in a neutral location."

Neutral location. The woman on the other end of the call made it sound as if they were about to negotiate some sort of a peace treaty, not discuss a problem he might be having with suddenly finding himself raising two rambunctious little boys.

But then, what did he know? Maybe this was the new approach to psychology. He was game for anything.

"Sure. Why not," Brady sportingly agreed. "Eleven o'clock tomorrow at Provisions," he repeated. "I'll be the harried-looking man on his way to having his hair turn prematurely gray."

Thinking he was trying to lighten the mood by joking, Harper laughed. She actually understood how he probably felt. Some of the fathers she had worked for in the past acted as if fatherhood was the hardest job in the world instead of the absolute joy it could be. To her way of thinking, it was her job, in part, to show them the way.

"All right, then, Mr. Fortune. I'll see you tomorrow at eleven," Harper said just before she hung up the receiver.

This was it, Harper thought, looking down at the phone. This could very well be the job she had been hoping for.

The long, frustrating dry spell might *finally* be over!

Her heart racing, Harper hurried over to the closet where she had hung up her small wardrobe to pick out just the right outfit for the meeting tomorrow. Aware that first impressions were everything, she needed to look her most competent for the interview.

The next day, Brady was surprised that he was nervous. He hadn't thought he would be, but he actually was.

It didn't matter, really. Even if the idea of talking to someone about his feelings made him uncomfortable, he reminded himself that this wasn't about him. He was doing it for the boys, to get a better handle on how he could give them the best life possible.

Maybe, he admitted, just maybe he was doing it for himself, too. So that he could manage to keep them all together, so that he could see the boys grow up to become young men.

Damn, Brady thought as he straightened his tie, life had become much too complicated in these last six months. But then, he thought, if things weren't complicated and confounding, he wouldn't have to be meeting with this Harper Radcliffe and the woman would probably be out of a job.

Brady sighed. He was overthinking this, he told himself. And overdressing as well, he decided, taking another look at himself in the full-length mirror. He looked as if he was dressed to meet some high-class dignitary—not a therapist.

He glanced at his watch. It was too late to change, he thought—unless he wanted to be late. And he knew if he was, Ms. Radcliffe would probably make some sort of a big deal out of that, claiming it was an unconscious attempt to demonstrate his superiority over her or some such nonsense.

No, he wasn't going to waste time changing into something more casual. Besides, maybe this woman would be impressed—or intimidated—by what he was wearing. Either way, it might wind up working in his favor.

And so would being on time for this meeting, Brady told himself as he left the house.

Right now, Brady was really grateful that he had gotten the twins registered yesterday. Because dragging the boys to this meeting might have proven to be difficult at best.

He didn't want to consider what it might have wound up being at its worst.

Brady did his best to bolster his confidence.

Maybe he'd even learn something, he thought as he drove to the restaurant.

What he needed to do was keep an open mind, Brady told himself. After all, that was why he had made the phone call to begin with, right? To learn something that he could actually use when it came to dealing with the twins—or possibly even learn what it was that he was doing wrong with them.

Because, to his way of thinking, by all rights, Toby and Tyler should have been calming down by now—shouldn't they? He had to be doing something wrong, he thought. Possibly even failing them. But how?

The question continued gnawing at him—and his gut—as he got out in the restaurant parking lot.

It suddenly occurred to him, as he walked toward the restaurant's entrance, that he should have asked for this woman's description. Otherwise, how was he going to recognize this person that Mrs. Ferguson had recommended to him? He didn't have a clue what this woman looked like. Until she had called him back, he hadn't even known that she *was* a woman.

Walking in through the restaurant's double doors, Brady stood in the entrance and looked around the restaurant.

How was he—?

Brady abruptly stopped as he stared into the dining area.

Wasn't that…?

The knockout he'd had coffee with at Roja yesterday—or had begun to have coffee with, he amended, recognizing the woman he had met.

What was she doing here, he wondered. This had to qualify as one hell of a coincidence, Brady couldn't help thinking. Unless…

And then it hit him like a ton of bricks.

Oh wow!

The knockout and the woman he was meeting were one and the same.

Harper saw him from across the room. The man who had bought her coffee yesterday because, according to him, he had needed to talk to someone. Then, as she proceeded to do just that, attempting to give him a little advice as well, the man had abruptly pulled back and walked out of the restaurant.

And then it suddenly hit her. *That* was why the man on the answering machine had sounded so familiar to her. It was *him*. The widower with the twins, she recalled.

He was the one she was meeting?

Wow, talk about it being a small world, Harper thought. They just couldn't make this kind of stuff up, she silently marveled, watching as the man from yesterday's abbreviated encounter at Roja began to walk toward her.

"Harper Radcliffe, I presume?" Brady asked as he came up to the table where she was seated.

For Harper's part, she smiled at him as she inclined her head.

"Brady Fortune," she said. Because it was the polite thing to do, she put out her hand to him. "Nice to formally make your acquaintance."

Brady took her hand in his. He couldn't help thinking how delicate it felt to him.

"Same here," he responded.

And then something in his head suddenly yelled *May-day*! He couldn't go through with this, Brady decided. "Although, I've thought it over," he told her, "and I've changed my mind."

Harper wasn't sure that she was following what he was saying to her, although part of her did have a very uneasy feeling that she knew. The man was dumping her before he even gave her a chance.

Why?

She pressed on, feigning ignorance.

"Changed your mind about what?" she asked him.

Brady was straightforward in his answer— or at least he thought he was. "About retaining your services."

Another person would have taken that as their

cue to leave. They would have stood up and just walked away with their dignity intact.

But another person wasn't as desperate as she was to be gainfully employed again. Employed in not just any field, but the field of her choice. As a nanny.

So rather than just pick up and leave, Harper decided to press the matter. "May I ask why?"

"Because I don't believe in them," he told her point-blank.

"You don't believe in *them*?" she repeated, utterly confused. What was that supposed to mean? And just what did he mean by *them*?

"Are you going to question and take apart everything I say?" Brady asked, not knowing whether he was offended or just confused.

"Sorry," she responded crisply. "I'm just trying to wrap my head around why a grown man is telling me that he doesn't believe in nannies."

Brady blinked, totally confused now. What was this woman talking about? "What?"

Okay, Harper thought, now this extremely handsome, infuriating idiot was just trying to bait her for some unknown reason. "Why you don't believe in nannies?" she repeated, enunciating every word slowly and clearly.

"I didn't say that," Brady insisted.

Harper took a deep breath, digging deep for the patience that served her well when she worked with children. This man was a real challenge, she thought.

"You just said you don't believe in what I do for a living. You referred to them as my *services*." Her eyes pinned him against the wall. "Are you with me so far?"

He stared at her, his confusion only growing. "What sort of a mind game is this?" he wanted to know. "Because if this is your way of trying to get me to spill my guts to you, well, it's failing. I'm just not about to do that."

Harper did a mental double take. He must have had a hell of a childhood, she couldn't help thinking. "Why would you want to do that anyway?" she questioned. She had absolutely no desire to be privy to this man's spilled "guts."

"Well, isn't that what you people want?" he challenged. "To get your would-be patient to share their so-called deepest, darkest secrets with you?"

"Okay, back up here," Harper told him, holding up her hands as if that would somehow physically make him stop talking. "What exactly do you mean by 'you people'?" she wanted to know.

"You," he said, gesturing at her. Then elaborated by adding, "Shrinks."

"Shrinks?" she repeated, staring at him. "The only thing I ever 'shrank,'" she informed the man sitting opposite her, "was a load of laundry when I wasn't accustomed to the washing machine."

And then she realized that it was all starting to make sense now. The man's hostility as well as his confusion, it all made sense.

"Are you telling me that you think I'm a psychologist—or a psychiatrist?" She wasn't sure which he was accusing her of being. The only thing she knew was that while she respected the vocations, she was neither of those professions.

"Aren't you?" he asked, beginning to feel just the slightest bit foolish. If this was a colossal mix-up, how did he fix it?

"Oh lord, no," Harper answered with a laugh. "If I were one, I'd probably be a little more together than I am now. Maybe a lot more together," she amended with a genial shrug.

Wow, talk about making a mistake, Brady thought, totally embarrassed now. He had just made a huge mistake by inserting not just his foot in his mouth, but both of them.

All the way in.

At the same time.

"Then what are you?" he asked, thinking back to the card that Mrs. Ferguson had pressed into his hand. The card with this woman's phone number on it. He'd thought that Mrs. Ferguson had believed he needed help and had mistakenly thought she was giving him the name of a psychiatrist to help him find his way out of this emotional maze.

"I'm a nanny," Harper told him. "I thought you knew that."

Brady shook his head. "There was nothing about you being a nanny on the card I was given. It had your name on it and the slogan 'Help when you need it.'" His eyes met hers. "That's not exactly crystal clear," Brady complained.

Harper closed her eyes. *Damn*, she thought.

When she opened them again, she said, "You're absolutely right. That was my fault. I should have been clearer." She made a mental note to redo her business cards.

Since she was being so nice about it, Brady was willing to share in the blame. "I guess I just read into it," he admitted.

Harper brightened. "Let's start all over again." She put out her hand to him. "Hello, I'm Harper Radcliffe and I'm a nanny currently between jobs. Would you have any interest in making use of my services?" she asked him.

For a second, he just stared at her. And then he smiled. Broadly. "You have no idea how much I would *love* to make use of your services, Ms. Radcliffe," he told her.

Maybe it was the fact that he had used the word *love* or maybe her last experience with her boss's husband had completely colored her reaction to men in general and she would have re-acted this way no matter what he said. In any case, Harper suddenly felt a cold wave washing over her, warning her that this had turned out to be a really bad idea.

To make matters worse, this man was just too damn handsome for either one of their own good. Besides, she had learned to be very wary of gorgeous men, predominantly because they were accustomed to getting their way whenever they wanted.

Taking a job with this man was just asking for trouble and she had had enough trouble, as far as she was concerned, to last her a lifetime.

"On second thought," Harper told the man before her, "I've decided that maybe we're not such a good match after all." She rose to her feet before the stunned Brady was able say anything in response. "Thank you, but no thank you."

And with that, Harper turned on her heel to walk out of the restaurant.

Chapter Six

"Wait, Harper—Ms. Radcliffe," Brady corrected himself, calling to the woman he had begun to think of as his potential lifesaver. "You're leaving?"

The way he said it, he sounded stunned, like someone surprised to find themselves being abandoned. Against her better judgment, Harper turned around and decided to give the man an extra minute before retreating.

"I'm afraid this isn't going to work out," she told him.

Brady continued to stare at her, totally at a loss. "But why are you turning this job down before you even meet Toby and Tyler?" he asked her. "Isn't that against the rules in the Nanny Handbook?"

He knew she needed the work. Why else would someone who was a professional nanny by trade have been looking into getting a waitressing job at Roja? It certainly couldn't have been the enticement of being on her feet for eight hours a day or more, carrying heavy trays and putting up with irate, irrational customers' complaints.

He waited for her to make him understand—or to change her mind about her decision.

Before Harper could frame any sort of a response to Brady's question, two young, pretty blondes who had obviously heard the exchange between her and Brady approached their booth.

And from the look on Brady's face, he recognized them.

Were they ganging up on her, Harper wondered.

"Brady, I thought I heard your voice," one of the women declared. She was obviously pleased to see him, but she appeared to also be concerned at the same time. "Is there something wrong?" she wanted to know, looking from him to Harper.

She looked down at the table. "It can't be the food. There's nothing here. Is it my waitress? Is she taking too long to bring you your order?" the woman asked.

Not waiting for an answer, her eyes shifted to Harper. She smiled and extended her hand. "Hello, I'm Ashley Fortune and this lovely creature next to me is my sister, Megan. We're Brady's cousins and the owners of this restaurant. And you are…?"

"Harper Radcliffe," Harper replied, feeling just a little awkward about the way the two women were regarding her.

Megan only had enough time to say, "Hi," To Harper before Ashley returned to what she viewed as the problem. "Is there anything I can do to make this a better dining experience for you?" she asked, looking at her cousin.

He knew that his cousin was referring to the food at the restaurant, but all Brady could think of was that he was losing his shot at getting a nanny—one that had come recommended by Mrs. Ferguson. And he still hadn't the slightest idea why that was happening.

Desperate, Brady glanced at both his cousins and said, "You can use those charms of yours to talk Ms. Radcliffe here into being the twins' nanny. Maybe if she came over to the house to meet them, she might change her mind about turning the job down."

It was a long shot, but it was the only one he had left, Brady thought.

Megan's face instantly lit up. "Oh my lord,

yes. Those sweet boys could definitely benefit from a woman's steady presence in their lives. You would be a virtual lifesaver, Ms....Radcliffe, is it?" Megan asked her, obviously uncertain if she had heard the last name correctly.

"Harper," the young woman being laid siege to said, feeling that using her last name in this case was a little too formal. "My first name is Harper."

"Well, Harper, how would you like to feel like the cavalry and ride to our cousin's rescue?" Ashley wanted to know. Not waiting for an answer, Ashley wiggled into the booth, sitting on Harper's left side.

Not waiting for an invitation, Megan immediately sat down on Harper's other side, immobilizing her in case she had any thoughts about making an escape before they convinced her to take the job their cousin was offering her.

Looking on, Brady decided that the young nanny probably didn't stand a chance against these two—at least he hoped she didn't because he *really* needed her. He had the good sense not to smile too broadly as he watched his cousins go to work.

"He's a really good guy," Ashley was telling the nanny. "He relocated here all the way from upstate New York because he needed help with his twins—well, they're not really *his* twins—" she corrected herself.

"They are in the eyes of the law," Megan pointed out. "Brady got legal custody of them when his friends—the twins' parents—died in that awful motorcycle accident," she quickly explained to Harper.

This was the first she was hearing about this. The fact that the man wasn't the twins' blood relative but was still taking on the task of raising them raised his stock in her eyes by a hundredfold. Maybe she had been too hasty, turning him down, she thought.

"But our confirmed bachelor here," Ashley told her as she gestured toward her cousin, "didn't have a clue how to get a puppy to listen to him, much less two overenergized four-year-olds. He thought family might help, but we're all busy trying to make a living, so we haven't had the time to be of much help with the twins," Ashley confessed with obvious genuine regret.

"Which brings us to you," Megan said. "Nannies are supposed to be able to get kids to jump through hoops and be on their best behavior, right?" she asked Harper, pinning her with a look.

Harper felt as if she was on the receiving end of a one-two punch. She laughed at the last thing Megan had said to her. The woman was being highly optimistic in her assessment of what a nanny could actually do, she thought.

"You have obviously either read or seen *Mary Poppins* one too many times," Harper told the two sisters.

Ashley looked genuinely disappointed. "So that's it?" she asked. "You're turning the job down without even meeting the kids?"

Megan jumped in then. "Oh, but you've got to meet the boys and give them a chance to steal your heart," she insisted, then added, "For all our sakes."

Okay, Brady thought, seeing his cousins do their act. They were laying it on thick. Too thick. This really wasn't fair.

"Ashley, Megan, you're ganging up on Ms. Radcliffe. Give her a chance to breathe," he told them. And then he turned what Harper could only describe as his beautiful, heartwarming brown eyes on her. She could feel herself melting. "All I ask is that, in all fairness, you come and meet Tyler and Toby before you decide to turn this job down."

Harper looked from one side to the other, taking in the three faces that were literally pleading with her to do the right thing.

To do the *only* thing that she was born to do, she reminded herself.

Ordinarily, she would have immediately jumped

at the chance. But she wasn't and she knew what was stopping her. Justine Wheeler's husband— or at least the memory of Justine Wheeler's husband—was what was causing her to second-guess this whole situation and actually shy away from it.

She was afraid of history repeating itself.

But this man who had met with her—according to her terms—was in dire need of someone to help him manage the twins he had unexpectedly gotten custody of. She couldn't allow that awful experience she had gone through with her boss's husband to keep her from what she had once regarded as her life's calling.

She was good at her job, damn it, and she needed to feel that way again. Needed it as much as apparently Brady Fortune appeared to need her.

Harper could feel herself coming around ever so slowly.

"Well, I'm still not sure I'm the right person for this job, but I'm not accustomed to being unfair," she told Brady. "So I will reserve judgment until I meet Toby and Tyler—"

She got no further. Megan threw her arms round her, hugging Harper hard.

"You won't regret this," Megan promised fiercely.

"Well, one thing's for sure," Brady told Harper. "I know that *I* won't regret this."

He would have hugged the person he considered to be the potential answer to all his prayers just the way that Megan had, but he had a feeling that doing so might just spook her enough to make her change her mind, so he remained where he was, sitting opposite Harper as well as his cousins in the booth.

Megan put it into words for all of them. "You're the answer to a prayer, Harper. Three prayers."

"Most likely even more than that if we could take an accurate head count. Everyone in Rambling Rose wants to help Brady with his newly acquired family," Ashley confessed. "But truthfully, in this situation, you're probably the only one who knows what she's doing."

Too much flattery had always embarrassed Harper. She was only doing what came naturally to her. "I wouldn't go that far," Harper told the three cousins, deflecting words of praise she felt she hadn't earned yet.

"I would," Brady freely admitted. "If you can get them to listen to you, you'll be doing better than I have in six months," he told her.

Harper cleared her throat. "All right then, you want to take me to meet your boys?" she asked, ready to leave the restaurant.

"More than anything in the world," Brady told her. As she began to rise, he caught hold of her wrist, anchoring her in place. "But they're in preschool right now and the last thing I want to do is disrupt their day." He smiled at the phrase he had inadvertently used. "They're perfectly capable of doing that all by themselves. But, like I said, they're in school right now. That gives us at least a couple of hours before I wind up bringing you before the firing squad."

"You're really not selling this, cousin," Ashley told him with a laugh.

Brady looked as if he knew he had made a mistake and wasn't sure just how to backtrack from it. His shrug was innocent. "I guess I was just being honest."

Harper found herself coming to his rescue. "Honesty is a very admirable quality." There was approval in her voice that she didn't have to feign.

"I will be as honest as you can bear as long as you promise to give the twins a chance," Brady told her in all sincerity.

She looked at him for a long moment, then nodded. He'd sold her. "Fair enough."

Ashley looked at her sister, relieved. "Well, our work here is done," she declared, beaming as she rose from the booth. Megan slid out from the other side. "Thank you," she repeated, looking at Harper. "Well, enjoy your lunch, you two—and oh, by the way," she added, squeezing Harper's hand, "Lunch is on me. Order anything you like. The sky's the limit," Ashley emphasized.

Taken aback, Harper said, "That's very generous of you."

"I just want to make you feel welcome here at our restaurant. You'll find that it's a very warm place," Ashley told her with a wink.

"Well, you certainly have made me feel welcomed," Harper told her. "Or guilty if I decide to turn the job down," she added, viewing the situation from the flip side.

Sitting back in the booth as his cousins took their leave, Brady observed, "You know, that's very astute of you."

He watched in fascination as an almost beatific smile slipped over her lips.

"I deal with children," Harper reminded him. "And children, bless 'em, can be positively the most manipulative little creatures on the face of the earth."

Tickled, Brady laughed, finding himself appreciating her view on the situation. "Something tells me you are most definitely the right woman for the job," he told her.

She wanted to stop him right now. "Let's not get ahead of ourselves," Harper warned. "We'll take this one step at a time."

"Right," Brady agreed. He proceeded cautiously. He didn't want to blow this now that it was finally happening. "Step one is ordering lunch," he reminded her. "And my cousin did say the sky's the limit."

"That was very generous of her," Harper told him as she scanned the menu she had just picked up.

"Well, we try to take care of each other in Rambling Rose," he told her.

"Apparently," she murmured, attempting to make a selection between the choices she had narrowed down to. "It must be nice to have such a big family."

"I never really thought about it," he admitted to Harper. "I mean, I didn't grow up with my Texas relatives, but I had five siblings—including a twin brother. So it was just something that was always a part of my life, but now that you mention it, I guess it is nice. Although," he told her, "there were times I really did want to be alone—and that's when life seemed to be the most crowded."

Spoken like a real bachelor, Harper thought. A bachelor, she was willing to bet, who wasn't through planting his wild oats. And, if she took this job being nanny to his newly acquired twins, that would leave him free to go on planting to his heart's content, she thought.

The next moment she told herself that wasn't her concern one way or the other. What *was* her concern, if she decided to take this job, was whether she and the boys meshed. Could she be a plus in their lives or would this turn out to be just a way for her to earn a salary?

If it turned out to be the latter, then she wouldn't take the job, Harper decided. Even though she needed it, it had never been about the money for her. Instead, it was what she could bring to the table and add to the lives of the children she took care of.

That was what was important to her.

"So, what will it be?" Brady asked, his voice breaking into her thoughts.

Rousing herself, Harper realized that she hadn't really heard him. "Excuse me?"

Brady held up the menu, drawing her attention to it. "Lunch," he prompted, tapping the dark green cover. "What did you finally decide to have?"

Her mind wasn't on food. At the moment, she was too preoccupied thinking about meeting the twins. But she didn't want to keep him waiting while she made up her mind about something as trivial as lunch.

"I can't make up my mind," Harper told him, not going into why she couldn't. "Why don't you choose for me?" she suggested.

Though she looked delicate, Harper Radcliffe didn't strike him as someone who abdicated her choices, even when it came to something as simple as ordering lunch.

"Are you sure?" he asked her. When she looked at him quizzically, he explained, "One of us could be a vegan, or have a food allergy, which means that the other person shouldn't be the one making the choices for lunch."

That was a really odd thing to say, Harper thought. "Well, I'm not a vegan," she told him. "As a matter of fact, I happen to really like eating meat."

"No kidding?" he asked, his face lighting up. One of the last few women he had gone out with—pretwins—had been a devout vegan. "So do I. I'm very partial to steak." Brady grinned. "Guess what, Ms. Radcliffe? I think that I just found something that we have in common."

Harper laughed. "I'm sure there are probably other things."

"I look forward to finding them out," he told her in all sincerity.

Uh-oh, Harper thought. There were red lights flickering inside her head.

"Tell you what, why don't we use this time to get to know a little about each other?" Brady suggested. "Over lunch," he elaborated, then added, "So I can get to know just what sort of a person I'm handing the care of my best friend's kids over to."

"That's why you want to get to know me better?" she asked, still not certain.

"It'll do for starters," he replied, his eyes meeting hers.

Harper felt something warm shimmying up and down her spine. Was that a sign of things to come? Or had her bad experience with Edward Wheeler managed to color the way she saw even the most harmless of comments? She didn't know. But for now, she decided to give Brady the benefit of the doubt.

She lowered her eyes to look at the menu. "I think I'm ready to order now," she told him.

He smiled and nodded. He'd figured she would be better off making her own choice.

Chapter Seven

As he drove home from the restaurant, Brady kept raising his eyes to look in the rearview mirror every few seconds.

He was relieved to see that Harper was still there, still following him in her unimpressive, fifteen-year-old four-door car just as she had told him she would.

Even so, Brady half expected to see the car make a U-turn and head back to wherever it was that Harper was currently living.

But mercifully, the woman he had wound up pinning all of his hopes on in the last couple of hours was still there. Still following him.

He was happy that she was actually willing to keep her word and meet with his kids.

Brady suddenly gripped the steering wheel harder as he realized the import of the thought that had just gone through his head.

His kids.

When exactly had that happened? Brady asked himself, clearly stunned.

When had he started thinking of Toby and Tyler as "his" kids instead of Gord's kids? Or even "the" kids? He had no answer for that, only that the term had somehow snuck up on him.

To give Harper's meeting with the twins a better chance of going well, he'd decided it should take place on his own home territory. Brady had asked his brother Kane to pick up the boys at the preschool when he went there to pick up his fiancée's daughter. Since Kane already had a set of his own keys to the house, Brady had asked Kane to bring the boys home and stay with them until he himself could get there with Harper.

He knew that his brother had to sympathize with what he was going through to some degree. Kane was soon to become an instant father himself when he married Layla, who came with a precious little girl in the bargain.

Nothing seemed to daunt Kane, Brady thought, checking in the mirror again to make sure that Harper's car was still behind him.

It was.

But then, Brady thought, both of his older brothers probably thought the same thing about him. That nothing daunted him.

He had certainly thought that about himself until six months ago. These days it was just a struggle to try to take everything in stride and not let things like cuts and scrapes, and broken glasses and plates, get to him. Lord knew it wasn't easy. Trying to get the twins to actually pay attention and listen to him when he told them to do something had shown Brady a whole new side of himself. A side that had turned out to be a great deal more flappable than he would have ever thought possible.

But after today, with any luck, things should be a lot calmer, he promised himself. All he had to do was convince a perfectly sane, rational woman that she'd actually enjoy living in a circus-like atmosphere where three-foot clowns ran the show.

No big deal, right?

As he drew closer to the new house he had recently purchased, again with the boys in mind, he saw Kane's car parked in his driveway. His brother had managed to get here ahead of him, he thought, even though he had been closer to it than Kane was.

Part of Brady had hoped to bring this nanny

into his house before all hell had a chance of breaking loose.

Brady wondered if this was the kind of situation where the term *trial by fire* had initially originated.

Instead of parking his car in the garage which was overloaded with boxes, both his and the boys', Brady decided it was simpler to just choose a spot in the driveway. He parked over to one side, making sure he left plenty of room for Harper's vehicle. It wasn't that her car was big, but it gave the impression that it was close to being on its last legs, which meant that it could very well die soon. When it did, it would need a lot of room to allow other vehicles to come and go easily.

After getting out of his car, he turned his attention toward helping guide Harper into a space away from both his car and Kane's.

It went a great deal better than he would have predicted.

Until his would-be nanny got out of her car. She didn't exactly look happy, he thought.

"Was all that gesturing you were doing your way of telling me that you don't think I'm capable of parking my car without damaging yours, or damaging whoever belongs to that one?" she asked, nodding toward Kane's truck.

He hadn't meant to insult her, Brady thought.

He supposed there was such a thing as over-thinking a situation.

Brady launched into damage control. "No, I guess I was just afraid that you were going to change your mind and tear out of here at the first sign of a problem."

"What kind of a problem?" she wanted to know, not following him. "Parking a car?" she asked, saying the first thing that came to her mind. "I've been driving since I was sixteen," Harper told him. "And the reason this car looks as if it's been driven in a demolition derby for the last ten years is because I bought it—very used—from a friend of mine after my car caught fire because of a defective fuel pump. Andrew was always hard on his cars," she said, mentioning the vehicle's previous owner by name.

Harper regarded the vehicle parked away from the other two vehicles. She had to admit that hers looked very much like a pariah. "It was all I could afford."

"You don't have to explain anything to me," Brady told her.

"I beg to differ. The look on your face says I do," Harper contradicted.

He was about to make another disclaimer about the situation when his front door suddenly flew open and both of the twins came racing out.

Toby and Tyler made a direct beeline for

Brady till they spotted the person standing next to him and abruptly stopped short.

"Who's this?" Toby wanted to know. He looked Harper up and down and apparently tried to size up the situation. Putting his little hands on his hips, Toby turned toward Brady and demanded, "Did you get married?"

"Is that why you had Unca Kane pick us up?" Tyler asked, not to be left out. "'Cause you were getting married?"

Kane came out, one hand wrapped around the hand of the brand-new addition in his life, a sweet little girl named Erin. "They heard the sound of your voice and got away from me before I could stop them," his brother admitted, slightly embarrassed.

"You don't have to apologize," Brady told him. "I appreciate you picking them up for me." Aware that everyone was looking at the woman with him, he quickly made the introductions. "Harper, this is my brother, Kane, and Erin. Kane, this is Harper Radcliffe."

While Erin hid behind Kane's legs, Kane leaned over and extended his hand to the young woman with his brother.

"Nice to meet you, Harper. I take it you're the one Brady thinks is going to bring order back to his chaotic life. Bless you for that," he added with a wide smile that Harper thought made him look a great deal like the man she had followed here.

"And these are the twins, Toby and Tyler," Brady told Harper, pointing at each of them in turn. "Boys, this might be your new nanny."

For just a moment, the twins were almost well behaved—and then they started firing questions at her, their young, high-pitched voices blending into a cacophony of dissonance.

Not wanting Harper to feel as if she was being hemmed in, not to mention overwhelmed, Brady said, "She hasn't made up her mind about the job yet, boys."

He was secretly pinning part of his hopes on the twins being able to tug at her heartstrings, and part on his own charm wearing her down. Although, he was ready to admit, that charm was beginning to wane somewhat. He just hoped that it was still strong enough to convince Harper to take on something she had supposedly professed to love doing.

Mentally crossing his fingers, Brady looked at her and asked, "Right?"

"Right," Harper answered, her expression giving nothing away.

Tyler still appeared to be stuck in first gear. Tugging on the bottom of Harper's blouse, he asked, "If you marry Unca Brady, does that mean you're our mommy?"

Toby frowned, taking on a superior air. "No, stupid, that makes her our aunt, right?" He looked up at Harper to back him up.

As Brady watched her, he felt as if he was observing Harper diving into the deep end of the pool. Squatting down to be on the same eye level as the twins, she addressed Toby. "Well, number one, I'm not marrying your Uncle Brady, and number two, you should never call your brother stupid."

"Why not?" Toby wanted to know. It was clear that the boy didn't like being given any sort of restrictions, even when it came to using words.

"What's number three?" Tyler piped up so as not to be ignored.

These boys were clearly going to be a test to her abilities, Harper thought. She could feel it. They were bright. Very bright.

Well, she did enjoy a good challenge, Harper mused philosophically. It made the whole experience that much more interesting.

Rising to her feet, Harper placed a hand on each small shoulder. "There is no number three," she told Tyler, then qualified, "—for now. But I'm sure there will be. Eventually. And you shouldn't call anyone stupid," she told Toby, "because everyone is smart in their own way."

Toby's frown deepened. "Stevie Jordan isn't smart," he told this new nanny.

"Oh, I think you're being too hard on this Stevie, Toby," Harper told him. "I think if you try, you can find something that Stevie is smart about or good at. You just have to think about it."

"Naw," Toby said, shaking his head as he waved a dismissive hand at the idea.

"Would you try?" Harper coaxed, looking into the boy's eyes. "For me?" she added, lowering her voice, one friend to the other.

And as Brady looked on, the twin he considered to be the more rambunctious one of the duo seemed to puff up his chest as he pretended to consider the pretty lady's request.

Brady realized that Toby was almost blushing as he replied, "Well, okay. For you."

Dumbfounded as well as very impressed, Brady looked at Harper. "Wow, I think I just witnessed a miracle." Unabashed admiration filled his eyes. "Anything you want, I'll pay it!" he promised the woman with heartfelt enthusiasm. "You have to take this job. Anything," he repeated. "Just name your price."

"I think he means it," Kane said as he began to make his way toward the truck, still holding on to Erin's hand. "I'd hold out for top dollar if I were you," he told Harper with a wink. "If Brady here can't pay it, the family will take up a collection.

"*Really* nice meeting you, Ms. Radcliffe,"

Kane told her again, shaking Harper's hand before he opened the rear door of his truck. "I hope I'll be seeing you here again," he said as he hoisted Erin up in his arms, then placed her in her car seat. He carefully made sure all the belts were secured. "Good luck, Brady," Kane called out to his brother before getting in behind the truck's steering wheel.

Nodding, Brady said, "Thanks again."

The next moment, his brother forgotten, Brady was looking at the woman he was trying to hire. Counseling himself to put one foot in front of the other, he crossed his fingers and looked at Harper.

"Why don't we go inside and you can get to know Toby and Tyler a little better?" he suggested. Everything was riding on this and so far, the twins hadn't blown it. He was hoping for another miracle.

Brady pushed the front door open a little wider. It was a not-too-subtle invitation to the woman who he was hoping would come around to seeing things his way.

"I'll go in," Harper agreed, "but I don't think I really need to get to know Toby and Tyler a little better," she told Brady.

What did that mean? Brady wondered, getting a sinking feeling in his stomach.

Oh damn, the twins have managed to some-

how torpedo this in record time, he thought. Back in New York, it had taken at least a day, and sometimes even more time, before the twins succeeded in doing something to make a babysitter or a nanny go running for the hills. But this, this had happened before Toby and Tyler even gave the woman any time to walk in the door.

"Are you sure?" Brady asked her, struggling to tamp down a desperate feeling. There had to be *something* he could say or do, he thought.

"Yes, I think so," she replied.

He could feel his heart sinking down to his toes. "Isn't there anything I could do or say to make you change your mind?" he wanted to know.

She looked at Brady, clearly confused. "Why would you want me to change my mind?"

Brady went for broke, feeling that at this point, he had nothing to lose. "Because, frankly, I need you, Ms. Radcliffe." Then realizing she might get the wrong idea—even though he did find himself attracted to her—he gestured toward the twins. "*They* need you," he said with emphasis.

"And?" she questioned.

"And?" Brady echoed quizzically, at a loss as to what was going on. "There is no *and*," he told her. "We *all* need you," he stressed. "It's as plain and simple as that."

Harper nodded her head. "I understand that."

"And you're still not going to take the job?" he asked, desperation gnawing at his insides.

Harper stared at him. "When did I say that?" she wanted to know.

He felt like someone who was doomed to go around in circles. "When you said that you didn't need to get to know them better," he pointed out.

"I *don't* need to get to know them better," Harper insisted, "because I've made up my mind."

The way she said it gave him a glimmer of hope, but he wasn't going to jump to any conclusion because it might be the wrong one in the end. It might wind up jeopardizing any chance he had left to get her to agree to work with the twins and turn them into little people. Little people who he had a prayer of ultimately helping nurture—safely—into adulthood.

So he asked, "To—?" and waited for Harper Radcliffe to say the right words. Words that would put his life back on track.

"—to accept your offer to become their nanny," Harper concluded.

"You have no idea what that means to me," he cried. Then, thinking that what he had just said might scare her, he quickly backtracked on his enthusiasm.

Or at least tried to. "I mean—"

Harper took pity on him and stopped Brady

before he could continue. "That's all right, I think I know what you mean and you're right, I do think that I can do some good here." She made eye contact with Toby and then Tyler in turn. "If you boys will let me," Harper told them sincerely.

It was obvious that Toby and Tyler weren't sure exactly what this new lady with the bright smile wanted them to do. But Harper could tell by the expression on their small, animated faces that they were willing to go along with almost anything—which was why she felt fairly confident that this would all go well once she and the boys became used to one another.

Brady knew that he was risking having this all fall apart on him, but he needed to make sure that this woman who had the power to turn everything around in his life understood exactly what was involved.

"You do realize that this is supposed to be a live-in position, right?" he asked her.

"It is?" He hadn't mentioned that earlier. Her last position had been a live-in one and that had ended badly. She didn't want a repetition of that.

"Is that a deal breaker?" he wanted to know, then started talking fast. "Because if it is, we can come to some sort of an arrangement for the time being," he said, desperate not to have her change her mind.

Harper looked at the twins' upturned faces, thinking over what Brady had just said. He was willing to be flexible. She could be the same.

"Why don't we do that?" Harper suggested. "We'll play this by ear to begin with. I'll come in every morning and stay until the twins are in bed and asleep," Harper told her new boss, smiling at the twins as she cupped each of their faces with one of her hands. "After that, we'll see how it goes."

"Is something going somewhere?" Tyler asked, perplexed.

"My sanity if your new nanny changes her mind," Brady said, looking at Harper with unabashed gratitude in his eyes.

"You're gonna stay?" the boys asked in unison.

"I'm going to stay," Harper confirmed.

The twins cheered, warming both her heart as well as Brady's.

Chapter Eight

"You wanna see my room?" Toby asked, although as far as he was concerned, it was a foregone conclusion that this new nanny did.

Not waiting for an answer, Toby wrapped his small and surprisingly strong fingers around Harper's hand and enthusiastically began pulling her toward the winding staircase.

"It's *our* room," Tyler told Harper indignantly, making a face at Toby as he corrected his twin. His small eyebrows drew together in an irritated V.

"He only sleeps there 'cause he's afraid of sleeping alone," Toby told Harper.

It was obvious that Toby didn't want this new

mother figure in his life to think that he was the baby of the pair.

"Am not!" Tyler insisted, clearly upset that Harper might believe Toby.

Rather than distance herself from this brewing argument, the way he would have—and had on occasion—as Brady watched the events unfold, Harper got into the middle of this scuffle quickly. And then managed to quell it.

"I'm sure your uncle Brady put you both in the same room so that you could keep each other company," Harper told the twins. "Trust me—it's really nice to have a brother around you can talk to when you have something you want to share."

Tyler slipped his hand into Harper's other hand, not wanting to be left out. He wanted to lead her up the stairs just like his twin.

"Do you have a brother?" he asked her eagerly. The more sensitive twin clearly wanted to learn everything there was about this new, special nanny his "unca" Brady had brought into their lives.

"I do. He's a soldier and halfway around the world right now," Harper replied. "But when we were kids, growing up, we would share secrets together." She smiled nostalgically. "You two are very lucky to have each other," she told the duo as she allowed them to take her up to their room.

"How come you think that's so special?" Toby wanted to know, making a face at Tyler. "I don't."

"Oh, you don't mean that," Harper told Toby. "And you're particularly lucky because you were each born with your best friend right there by your side. I think that's really special," she said.

Toby's lower lip curled. "Yeah, well, maybe," he was willing to guardedly admit.

For his part, Tyler shrugged a little too carelessly. "Toby's okay, I guess," he said.

Standing at the bottom of the stairs, watching this unfold, Brady could only marvel at his good luck. After what felt like an endless parade of countless nannies who had passed through his life, it looked as if he had finally, *finally* struck gold.

This woman was nothing if not the answer to a prayer, he thought.

Very honestly, part of him was afraid that he was dreaming. Brady was even tempted to pinch himself just to make sure he wasn't.

But then, if he was dreaming, he really didn't want to wake up.

The next moment, Brady thought of going upstairs just in case Harper ran into any trouble.

But then, he told himself that maybe it was better this way.

Barring any screams or cries for help, Brady decided to keep out of this, at least for the first couple of minutes or so. As much as he wanted this woman to stay—she gave off a competent air, the twins seemed to take to her instantly and added to that, Harper Radcliffe was extremely easy on the eyes—Harper needed to know what she was up against.

In all fairness, Toby and Tyler didn't mean to do half the things they did. He'd learned that about them. They were just being…boys, he thought with a resigned sigh. Then again, when he thought about some of the escapades he and his twin brother Brian had gotten into as kids, he supposed he should consider himself lucky.

It was up to him to make sure they didn't kill themselves while they were doing it. And an important part of that involved having him find the right person to be their nanny. He couldn't be with them 24/7. He needed to earn a living so that he was able to pay expenses for the three of them.

Brady glanced at his watch. It had only been five minutes, but it was way too quiet up there. Quiet made him even more nervous than the sound of screaming and the loud, jarring noises of things falling or being thrown.

Okay, he told himself. They had had enough time together. It was time to rescue Harper while there was hopefully still someone left to rescue.

Brady took the stairs two at a time, a sense of urgency mounting inside him with every step.

By the time he reached the landing, Brady was braced for the worst. He had once walked in on the twins tying up one of their nannies. The furious words that came flowing out of that woman's mouth were very far from PG rated.

The moment he managed to free her, the woman had stormed out of the apartment, threatening him with a lawsuit.

The lawsuit never materialized and he could only think that angry nanny wasn't able to find a lawyer who would stop laughing at her long enough to take on the woman's case.

He'd lucked out then, Brady thought. But there were only so many miracles allotted to a person and he couldn't separate himself from the idea that he had already exhausted his supply.

Still, it didn't keep him from hoping.

The door to the twins' room was open.

As he drew closer, Brady heard the sound of Harper's voice. She wasn't yelling or even telling the twins that they had to stop doing something.

She was reading, he realized. Reading a story to the twins. And for once, neither of the boys was offering a running commentary or their own version of what was being read to them.

The twins were actually being quiet—without being gagged, he thought in amazement.

Brady reached their room and saw that the twins were sitting on their beds, looking totally enthralled with the story that Harper was reading to them.

Gina had bought that book for them, Brady suddenly recalled. It was one of the last things the twins' mother had done before she had ridden off on the back of Gord's motorcycle, along with her husband, into eternity.

Brady remembered attempting to read the book to the twins just once, only to be stopped by Toby who refused to be quiet long enough for the story to be read.

Even Tyler had piped up, crying out, *That's mommy's book. You can't read it. Nobody can read it. Just Mommy*, he had tearfully insisted.

Brady had left the book on the shelf then, thinking that when the boys were older, maybe one of them would want to read it, even though it was clearly a fairy tale written for children and they, by then he assumed, might be a good deal older.

Suddenly he heard Tyler asking, "Why would that guy give Jack some old beans for his mommy's cow?"

Toby, ever practical in his own way, had a more immediate question. "Why didn't the beans squish in his pocket?"

"That's a very good question," Harper told

Toby. "Why do you think they didn't squish in his pocket?"

No doubt wanting to have Harper praise him too, Tyler raised his hand to get her attention. "'Cause they were magic beans, right? That's why they didn't squish, 'cause they were magic. Right?"

Harper smiled at Tyler. "You're absolutely right, Tyler. You boys are both very, very smart. I see that I'm going to have to work super hard to keep up with you two guys."

Tyler immediately took her words to heart. "Don't worry, I'll slow down for you," he promised.

Not to be outdone, Toby joined in. "Yeah, me, too. I'll go slow. Real slow," he emphasized.

Harper looked from one twin to the other, her hand on her chest in a show of how touched she was by their "sacrifice."

"You would do that for me?" she asked.

"Uh-huh!" Toby told her, nodding his shaggy head up and down.

"We sure would!" Tyler told her. Then, seeing Brady in the mirror over their bureau, Tyler swung around to look at his guardian standing in the doorway. "Can she be our nanny, Unca Brady?"

"Yeah, can she? We like this one," Toby added. "She's nice."

Harper had already agreed to be their nanny, but obviously the twins wanted to verbalize their approval. Brady laughed as his eyes met Harper's. "You have no idea how high that praise really is," he told the woman. "These two 'angelic' looking boys have sent so many nannies running for the hills that I've completely lost count. I can't tell you how happy I am that you decided to take this job."

"Me, too," Tyler told her, beaming up at Harper.

"Me, three," Toby cried, not to be outdone.

"Well, I do love a challenge." Harper affectionately tousled each boys' hair. "Have you boys eaten yet?" she asked them.

"Uh-uh," Tyler answered, shaking his head, sending soft brown hair flying back and forth around his sweet cheeks.

"Nope," Toby said with emphasis.

"Why don't you boys show me to the kitchen so I can look in the refrigerator and see what we can whip up together for dinner?" Harper suggested.

"You're beating up food?" Toby asked excitedly.

Harper struggled not to laugh. She didn't want to hurt anyone's feelings. "*Whip up* in this case means *cook*," she explained.

Toby cocked his head, as if that would help

him understand things better. "We're going to *cook* dinner?" he asked skeptically.

"Yes, we are. It's never too early to learn," Harper assured the boy.

"I wanna learn," Tyler told her, hoping not to be left behind.

"That's good because I'm going to need your help. *Both* of you," she said to the twins.

As she spoke, Harper was keenly aware that Brady was slowly circling around her, giving her an elaborate once-over. One she knew she wasn't meant to ignore. "Can I help you with something, Mr. Fortune?" she asked, turning to face him.

"No. I'm fine," he told her. "I'm just looking for wings."

Harper blinked. "Wings?"

"She's not a bird, Unca Brady," Tyler told him. "She's our nanny."

"I know she's not a bird," Brady said, not looking away from Harper. "But angels have wings, too. I was just looking for Ms. Radcliffe's wings."

"Who's Ms. Radcl—radcl—Ms. Rad?" Toby finally asked, settling on the only part of the name he could manage.

"She is," Brady told the twin, nodding toward Harper.

"No, she's not. She's Harper," Toby said. "She

said so." Big blue eyes turned toward the woman for confirmation. "Right?"

"You can't call her by her first name, Toby," Brady told the boy.

"I can't?" Toby asked, surprised and confused. "Why not?"

"No, it's okay, really," Harper assured her new employer. "*Radcliffe* is just too much of a mouthful for a four-year-old."

Toby drew himself up to look taller. "I'm almost five," he told her.

"Oh, my mistake," Harper apologized. "For an 'almost' five-year-old," she told Brady, restating her comment. "So unless it really makes you uncomfortable," she told Brady, "the boys can call me Harper. I'm fine with that."

No, he wasn't uncomfortable with it, but he wasn't the one who mattered here. This was between Harper and the twins. A soldier knew when to retreat—and Brady considered himself a good soldier.

"If it's okay with you, it's fine with me," Brady told her.

"Okay, now that that's settled," Harper said, turning back to the twins, "why don't we go see about making dinner?"

Tyler's eyes were shining in anticipation of what lay ahead. "Yeah, why don't we go see about making dinner!" he cried, echoing Harper's words.

Feeling like she was almost surrounded by the twins who were shifting around her and moving from side to side, Harper went to the kitchen.

Crossing to the refrigerator, she opened both doors at the same time. Considering its size, it had very little to offer on the inside.

She found a small block of sharp cheddar cheese, less than half a package of sliced ham, a few eggs and two peppers, one red, one green. Both were one day away from being on their way out.

Harper was studying the contents a moment too long, causing Toby to make a suggestion. "Maybe we can call 'takes out.'"

Still holding the doors open, she glanced down at the pint-sized assistant who had spoken last. "Takes out?" she questioned.

"Yeah," Toby told her, happy to be able to offer his help. "Unca Brady calls a place and then he takes it out when they come here with it. Takes out," he repeated for emphasis.

Harper pressed her lips together to keep from laughing. She had the feeling she was going to be doing that a lot.

She glanced over toward Brady, who spread his hands wide for her benefit, indicating that the process Toby had just told her about was a pretty frequent one for them.

"I see," she told the boys. "Well, I don't think we need to call for 'takes out' yet."

"We're going to eat that?" Tyler asked doubtfully, scowling into the refrigerator.

"You're going to eat frittatas," Harper informed the twins.

"Fer-what-as?" Toby wanted to know, his tone indicating that he didn't like the sound of that.

"I think I can show you better than I can explain it," Harper said, "But the idea behind it is to take a bunch of things you find in the refrigerator, put them all together and mix them up with eggs to make one big tasty meal," she concluded, simplifying the process for the twins as much as possible.

Toby still made a face. "Doesn't sound very good," he complained.

"It tastes better than it sounds," Harper assured the boy.

Toby continued to show his disapproval. "It'll have to," he said.

"Toby." There was a warning note in Brady's voice.

"No, no, that's okay," Harper told Brady, coming to Toby's defense. "He's entitled to his opinion. Just as I'm entitled to try to get him to change his opinion. And tomorrow," she informed Brady, "while the boys are in preschool, I'm going to go shopping to get this to look like an actual refrigerator instead of a holding zone for things about to go bad. And you boys are going to help me make this—" she gestured into the refrigerator "—into a good meal."

While Toby and Tyler vied for position so each one could exclusively offer his willing hands to the new nanny, the look on Brady's face told her that she was going to live to regret what she had just said.

In fact, she had two challenges, Harper thought. The first was getting the twins involved without becoming a danger to themselves, and the second challenge came in the form of getting Brady to retract that smug, sexy smile of his.

Harper was fairly certain that she was up to both challenges.

"Okay, boys, let's get to this," she said in a voice that all but declared, *Let the games begin*.

Chapter Nine

The moment Harper set out all the ingredients she intended to use to make this very first family meal, she could see Toby eyeing the knife lying on the table beside the scarred cutting board. She had been a nanny long enough to know an accident that was waiting to happen.

Moving quickly, her hand covered the knife handle before Toby could grab it.

Looking at him, she judged that his small face must have fallen at least half a foot. But it was also obvious to Harper that the more active twin didn't intend to give up easily.

"You said you wanted me to help," Toby whined, pouting.

"And you will," Harper assured him. Her eyes swept over the little people on either side of her. "Both of you," she stressed, then looked down at the boys' hands. "But I think you and your brother are pretty set on keeping all your fingers just the way they are and that's a really sharp knife." Harper lowered her voice and added conspiratorially, "I'm cautious about using that knife myself."

"What's caw-caw—that word?" Stymied, Toby surrendered his efforts to pronounce the word he had heard her use correctly.

"It means being super careful," Harper told the twin. "See this?" She held up her left hand and pointed out what looked like an old, curved scar right at the base of her thumb.

"Yeah?" Toby answered as Tyler all but moved into his shadow to take his own look at the scar. Both boys appeared fascinated.

"I did that when I was ten years old," Harper told them. "I was trying to cut a small piece of ham for a snack when the knife slipped and I wound up cutting my thumb."

"Did it hurt?" Tyler asked her. The look on his small face was the very picture of sympathy.

"Oh, it hurt like crazy," Harper told the more sensitive of the twins.

"And did you bleed?" Toby wanted to know, his eyes wide with anticipation.

The truth was that there had been a lot of blood. She still remembered being queasy, but that wasn't something she felt she should go into for a number of reasons. So all she said was, "Uh-huh," then changed direction. "Now, if we're going to make this dinner" she continued, "this is going to be a team effort—but I head the team." She let her words sink in. "Agreed?"

Two shaggy heads bobbed up and down, slightly out of sync.

"Agreed," the boys all but eagerly proclaimed in unison.

While this minidrama was unfolding, Brady was standing off to the side in the doorway, observing everything as it happened. He found himself in awe at how deftly Harper handled all this.

Harper Radcliffe, where have you been all my life? he silently asked in unadulterated admiration.

Feeling that this nanny-miracle worker might want her space to continue to weave her magic in peace, Brady withdrew from the kitchen entrance altogether. He crossed his fingers that whatever was happening at the moment would continue to go on happening.

"Can I get you anything?" Brady asked the twins' new nanny much later that evening, after

Toby and Tyler had finally settled down and gone to sleep. Dinner had been a huge success and far tastier than he had anticipated. Harper had just now finished cleaning up the mess left over from preparing dinner. Brady looked around the kitchen, clearly impressed with how neat everything appeared.

The woman was a wizard, he decided. She was definitely a pleasant change from some of the nannies who had been there before her. "Coffee? Tea? A life-long contract?"

Harper laughed, taking one last look around the kitchen to make sure she hadn't overlooked anything. "No, I'm good," she told Brady.

"You certainly are," he agreed with no small enthusiasm. He said it with such feeling that Harper looked at him in surprise. He realized that he needed to clarify himself before she misunderstood. "You have no idea what a breath of fresh air you are after the army of less-than-satisfying babysitters and nannies who have trooped through the twins' lives."

Not wanting to say anything negative about the women her employer had previously hired—especially without being privy to more information—Harper speculated, "They probably just had their own take on how things should be managed."

Recalling certain incidents, Brady frowned,

but decided it was best not to rehash bad times. Moving forward was far more advisable.

"To be honest, I didn't know what to expect. I just knew what didn't work. Until I witnessed you in action. Just so you know, you have a position here for as long as you want it." He laughed softly to himself, thinking of the twins. "For life if it comes to that."

It was Harper's turn to laugh. "I doubt very much that those boys are going to want a nanny hanging around when they turn eighteen, but it's nice to know that I've found steady employment— at least for the time being."

Brady nodded, although he couldn't help wondering why this petite miracle worker was being so cautious in her response.

He nodded toward the sofa. "You know, given the day you just put in, you're welcomed to put your feet up and unwind," Brady told her. He wanted her to feel comfortable here.

"If you don't mind, I'll take a rain check," she told her new employer. Hoping he wouldn't take offense, she explained, "It's been a long day. I'd just like to go home and get some sleep."

Brady felt an unexpected twinge of disappointment, which surprised him. But he managed to respond well. "Whatever you say," he told her. "You're the boss," he added with a smile.

Looking at him, Harper could literally feel her

heart skip a beat. *Get a grip, Harper. Remember Justine Wheeler's husband...*

Stop it, she chided herself. *Brady's nothing like that man*, Harper silently insisted, remembering the man who had caused her all that grief. But comparing the new with the old, she reminded herself, did a disservice to both Brady and the new job she had taken on.

A job she knew she was lucky to find after the depressing spate of time she had just gone through, searching for employment in both her field—and then out of it.

Don't blow this just because you're afraid of history repeating itself, Harper warned herself. *Yes, Brady Fortune is good-looking and charming. That doesn't mean that he's a reptile, eager to jump your bones the first chance he gets. You can't allow Wheeler to spook you that way*, Harper reprimanded herself.

She knew she was being logical and making sense, but that didn't make this any easier for her. Harper still couldn't help feeling nervous and uneasy being around Brady. She was hoping that once she got into some sort of a daily routine with the twins, this uneasiness would eventually fade away.

At least she could hope for the best, Harper thought as she left his house and drove to her very small studio apartment.

It took her an incredible amount of time to wind down. Every time she finally managed to doze off, visions of her new employer's sexy smile would make her eyes fly open as her heart pounded wildly.

She barely managed to get any rest at all.

"Did you sleep well?" Brady asked the following morning. He was coming into the kitchen to grab a cup of coffee before he got started with his day. He was surprised to find Harper was already there, preparing breakfast.

Harper looked over her shoulder. She noticed that instead of casual clothes, Brady was wearing a suit. He looked very dashing, as if he was ready to take off somewhere. She bit her tongue not to say anything about his appearance. She didn't want to do anything to create the wrong impression.

Which also meant not mentioning what had turned out to be a relatively sleepless night, a detail best kept to herself rather than risking having Brady read something into that, too.

"Yes, thank you," Harper responded cheerfully to his inquiry. Nodding at the frying pan, she said, "I'm making breakfast."

"I can tell," Brady teased. Assuming she was making it for the twins, he told her, "The boys'll be hungry when they get up."

"And you?" she asked pointedly. "What can I make for you?"

He indicating the coffee machine and the full pot. "Coffee'll do fine."

She gave him a reproving look. "Can't start a day on just coffee."

Brady responded with a laugh. "Well, with these guys, I haven't had the time to think of extra things like making myself breakfast. Getting Toby and Tyler fed was enough of a challenge for me to face first thing in the morning."

She couldn't help thinking that he cut an impressive figure in that suit he was wearing. "So, now that I'm here, you thought you'd go formal?" she asked, doing her best to sound serious.

"Oh, this?" he said, looking down at his attire. He'd forgotten all about the suit he'd put on. "Since you're here, I don't have to look for a sitter for the kids and I can finally go and get up to speed at the hotel," he explained, then added a footnote for her edification. "The Hotel Fortune is run by my cousins and they're putting me to work at the concierge desk."

"Not on an empty stomach they're not," she informed him decisively.

Harper's response surprised him. "You sound like my mother," Brady told her.

"I'll take that as a compliment," she said, adding, "Call it a by-product of being a nanny all these years. Now sit." Harper pointed to the chair at the head of the table. "Since I started making breakfast before you came down, it's ready," she told him, anticipating what he was about to say. "You can't complain that you don't have time to wait because you don't *have* to wait. Voilà," Harper declared, placing the plate of scrambled eggs, toast and bacon in front of him. "And yes, the coffee is ready, too," Harper told him, quickly pouring a cup for him and placing that next to the plate.

She might have anticipated what he wanted to say, but not what came afterward.

"Join me?" Brady asked, nodding at the chair opposite his.

Harper glanced at the mug of coffee she had poured for herself earlier. She had kept taking small sips of the brew while she worked.

"Okay," she agreed, bringing the mug over to the table, "but just for coffee. I've got two small tornadoes to beat to the punch."

Brady laughed.

"I probably shouldn't say that," she amended. "Let me rephrase. I want to be upstairs and getting the boys up before they have a chance to come bounding out of bed and get rolling on their own," she told him instead.

The idea of actually waking the twins up voluntarily seemed totally foreign to him. "I always

Dear Reader,

I am writing to announce the launch of a huge **FREE BOOKS GIVEAWAY**... and to let you know that YOU are entitled to choose up to FOUR fantastic books that WE pay for.

Try **Harlequin® Special Edition** books featuring comfort and strength in the support of loved ones and enjoying the journey no mader what life throws your way.

Try **Harlequin® Heartwarming™ Larger-Print** books featuring uplifting stories where the bonds of friendship, family and community unite.

Or TRY BOTH!

In return, we ask just one favor: Would you please participate in our brief Reader Survey? We'd love to hear from you.

This FREE BOOKS GIVEAWAY means that we pay for *everything!* We'll even cover the shipping, and no purchase is necessary, now or later. So please return your survey today. You'll get **Two Free Books** and **Two Mystery Gifts** from each series to try, altogether worth over **$20!**

Sincerely

Pam Powers

Pam Powers
For Harlequin Reader Service

Complete the survey below and return it today to receive up to 4 FREE BOOKS and FREE GIFTS guaranteed!

FREE BOOKS GIVEAWAY
Reader Survey

1
Do you prefer stories with happy endings?

◯ YES   ◯ NO

2
Do you share your favorite books with friends?

◯ YES   ◯ NO

3
Do you often choose to read instead of watching TV?

◯ YES   ◯ NO

YES! Please send me my Free Rewards, consisting of **2 Free Books from each series I select** and **Free Mystery Gifts**. I understand that I am under no obligation to buy anything, as explained on the back of this card.

❑ **Harlequin® Special Edition** (235/335 HDL GQ2U)
❑ **Harlequin® Heartwarming™ Larger-Print** (161/361 HDL GQ2U)
❑ **Try Both** (235/335 & 161/361 HDL GQ26)

FIRST NAME   LAST NAME

ADDRESS

APT.#   CITY

STATE/PROV.   ZIP/POSTAL CODE

EMAIL ❑ Please check this box if you would like to receive newsletters and promotional emails from Harlequin Enterprises ULC and its affiliates. You can unsubscribe anytime.

SE/HW-820-FBG21

thought it was criminal to wake them up. I was confident that they'd be up and creating havoc soon enough."

Harper smiled at his honesty. In his defense, she could see where he was coming from. "I guess we have different approaches. Mine works for me."

Brady could only shake his head. "More power to you, Ms. Radcliffe." He saw her wrinkling her nose. "What is it?" he asked, waiting for her response.

It wasn't what he anticipated.

"Given the close proximity that we'll be working in, I think you should call me Harper. It's less formal," she told him.

Brady had always found that he was usually able to read people—at least he could before this bombshell had exploded in his life. After all, he'd had no clue that his late best friend had made him the guardian of his twins—certainly not until all of this had engulfed him, blotting out his old life.

In Harper's case, he had thought that calling her by her first name was a liberty that would spook her and cause her to step back. Obviously he was wrong there, too.

"I didn't want to take any liberties that might make you feel uncomfortable," he explained.

Maybe she had misjudged him. For that matter, maybe he was more sensitive than she had given him credit for.

"I appreciate that," she told him, her eyes smiling at him. "But *Harper* will do just fine. Calling me Ms. Radcliffe makes me feel like an old schoolmarm out of the 1890s."

"Can't have that," Brady agreed. And then what he was putting in his mouth registered belatedly with his brain. He looked at his fork in wonder, as if he hadn't really been paying attention to what Harper had prepared for him. "Damn but this is good. I know it's only scrambled eggs, but this doesn't taste like any scrambled eggs I've ever had before. What did you do to them? And moreover, have you ever thought of opening up your own restaurant?" he asked as he took another big bite of his serving.

Brady watched as the smile on her lips seemed to take over every inch of Harper's face. "And call it what?" she asked, amused. "Eggs Galore? No. That's a very nice compliment," she responded, "but I'm very happy being a nanny. As a matter of fact, when I had to stop being a nanny, those were the longest, emptiest three months of my life." Although she had always longed for a family with all the trimmings, she had learned that wanting and having were two different things. Much to her dismay, love had never found her. That was the main reason she had initially decided to fill the emptiness by becoming a nanny.

Brady realized that he had no idea what had transpired to bring that hiatus about.

He knew that he thought of Harper as a great nanny because he had witnessed her with the twins and was impressed with both her creativity and her ability to all but pull a rabbit out of a hat. She didn't seem to get flustered by anything that the dynamic duo came up with. As a matter of fact, she was utterly unflappable.

But he still wanted to know what had happened to separate her from the vocation she professed to love since she *did* clearly love it.

"Just what happened to your last position?" he wanted to know. "You didn't mention it."

She took a breath. Incidents and details crowded her mind, jockeying for position. She wasn't up to putting them in order, nor did she want to remember them—not yet.

"Long story," Harper told him evasively, then reminded Brady, "and you did say that you were in a hurry."

Brady knew evasion when he encountered it and grinned at Harper.

"Yes, I did, didn't I?" And he really was. Finished eating, he rose from his chair. "But this isn't over," he informed her. "You've aroused my curiosity, Harper Radcliffe," he told her. "When

I get home tonight, you'll have to tell me what went down that wound up separating you from a job you obviously love."

Harper was not about to be honest with him and tell him about the obnoxious octopus that had been her employer's husband—a little fact that didn't keep him from making more and more uninvited advances on her.

Instead, she forced a smile to her lips. She had the next eight hours to come up with a believable story, she thought as she watched her new employer walk out the front door.

With any luck, that would be enough time.

Either that, or maybe he would even forget about asking her about it by then.

Chapter Ten

Callum Fortune stood back and covertly observed his cousin go through his paces at the Hotel Fortune concierge desk for the good part of an hour.

Finally stepping forward, Callum came up to the desk and openly complimented Brady. "From the moment I first laid eyes on you, I just had this feeling that you were going to work out."

The Hotel Fortune had been Callum's latest project. Something he had undertaken with the hope of bringing even more tourism to Rambling Rose.

A real estate developer and contractor by trade, Callum and his siblings involved in Fortune Brothers Construction had been experiencing a great deal of success in their efforts to build up the small Texas town of Rambling Rose a section at a time. Their pediatric center, veterinary clinic, upscale retail stores, wellness spa, and farm-to-table restaurant had all been well-received by the locals and were doing quite well.

Which was why the pushback against the luxury hotel Callum had wanted to proceed with next had been such an unexpected, unpleasant surprise. But it turned out that the down-to-earth locals resented such a large-scale project being forced down their throats—or at least that was how the residents of Rambling Rose viewed the idea of an unwanted "monstrosity" being built in their midst.

After much negotiating, a level of understanding between the two sides was finally reached, thanks in no small part to the intervention of Callum's cousin—and Brady's older brother—Kane, as well as Rodrigo Mendoza, the restaurant consultant for Provisions who had ultimately contributed his expertise to the hotel, too. Rodrigo was also engaged to Callum's sister Ashley, the general manager of Provisions. Thanks to his experience, Rodrigo had a little more insight into the locals' reactions to the original building plans—and had been able to convince Callum to scale back.

After all the protests were aired and reviewed, Callum and his siblings wound up designing a more welcoming and homey, albeit upscale, boutique hotel than they'd originally planned. But it was well worth their efforts.

After its official opening last month on Valentine's Day, the Hotel Fortune was a certified success. Though Callum had hired a general manager, he still made it his business to check in on the operation of his pet project. Today that meant observing their new concierge.

Granted, Brady had no experience in that area, but he had managed a sporting goods store, so he was no stranger to management and thinking on his feet. In addition he had good business sense.

The best part of all, in Callum's opinion, was that Brady had more than a little charisma. And that, he knew, was something that couldn't be taught. A person either had it or he didn't and that came in quite handy when dealing with guests.

After watching his cousin in action after a hotel guest came down to register a complaint about her accommodations and then left with a smile on her face, Callum knew that he had hired the right person for the job.

"You're a natural, Brady," Callum told his cousin, well pleased.

"Just grateful for a chance to prove myself—

and earn a living," Brady replied modestly. "I've got mouths to feed now."

He had learned not to allow compliments to go to his head. The last six months had taught him that fate was mercurial. He was determined to keep one eye on the prize and one eye on the future. It wasn't just about him anymore. He had the twins depending on him and he couldn't lose sight of that.

Wrapped up in getting Hotel Fortune off the ground and up and running, Callum had gone off track about that. "Right," he said with a nod. "How are the twins doing these days? I've heard some pretty hair-raising stories," Callum added with a hearty, amused laugh.

Brady leaned in a little closer, not wanting his voice to carry. "Quite frankly, it's one big balancing act," he admitted.

"I can give you the name of a babysitter if you need one," Callum offered.

He was fairly certain that he and his wife could share a contact or two that they trusted to watch their two-year-old girls. After all, he didn't want to risk losing Brady since his cousin seemed to fit so well into this new position.

"Thanks," Brady demurred, "but it looks like I won't be needing a sitter."

Callum grinned. He was really feeling good about the hotel. Things were finally all coming together and he could afford to relax just a little. Even laugh a little if the situation called for it.

"I didn't know you dabbled in black magic," he said to his new concierge.

Brady picked up on Callum's inference and got a kick out of it. "No black magic. I lucked out and hired this fantastic nanny."

"Fantastic, eh?" Callum raised his brow, instantly picking up on his cousin's enthusiasm.

"She is absolutely incredible with the twins," Brady said with gusto. "She had them both eating out of her hand within minutes. I never saw anything like it. I don't know how she does it," he said quite honestly, "but I am definitely going to make sure I hold on to her."

"As long as you don't wind up *actually* holding her," Callum warned.

Brady looked at his cousin, puzzled. "I'm not sure I follow you."

"I've learned that business and pleasure don't always mix," Callum cautioned. "If this nanny is an answer to a prayer, as you seem to indicate, I'd make damn sure I didn't do anything to rock that boat—or you risk this nanny handing in her notice. These are very tense times, cousin. Even the most innocent of moves run the risk of being misunderstood and since you've indicated that you're very pleased with what this nanny brings to the table and manages to do to keep your world running well, I'd make sure that your positions of employer and employee don't wind up getting blurred."

Funny that his cousin should mention that, Brady thought. Because if he was being strictly honest about it, he would have to admit that he was attracted to his boys' nanny.

Very attracted.

But Callum was right. The last thing he wanted to do was throw a monkey wrench into the works and risk losing someone whom the twins responded to and obviously liked. No possible, fleeting romantic tryst was worth that. Not when Harper Radcliffe could afford him the peace of mind that the dynamic duo were being looked after and well taken care of.

Brady flashed a smile at his cousin and employer. "Message received. Loud and clear," he assured Callum. "Besides, I wouldn't want to wind up confusing those energetic little rug rats about where Harper and I stand."

"Harper?" Callum questioned.

"That's the nanny's name. Harper Radcliffe," Brady told his cousin. "I actually find myself daydreaming about being able to look forward to some sort of a routine in the coming days—other than here at the hotel," he qualified.

Callum laughed. "I see that your requirements are really low—not including the hotel," he added with an amused smile.

"Oh, on the contrary, Callum. My requirements are very high. You weren't there for these last six months," Brady told his cousin. "My entire life went from carefree to chaos." He stifled a shiver as he recalled certain instances. "Make no mistake about it, this woman is worth her weight in pure gold—maybe even platinum."

Callum sympathized with his cousin. He didn't know if he would have had the stamina that Brady did. And once again, he had to give credit to his wife, who was herself a single parent to young twins when they met. Still, he couldn't resist poking fun at Brady. "Don't take this the wrong way, Brady, but whatever you do, don't let this Harper person suspect that you feel that way or you'll wind up turning your whole paycheck over to her every week."

Despite the humorous tone, Brady found himself getting defensive for Harper's sake, although, quite honestly, he wasn't sure what that was all about. "I don't think she's the type to take advantage."

"Well, for your sake, I really hope you're right," Callum told him. "But be careful. You don't know her all that well."

"I've entrusted that woman with the lives of two little boys. *My* two little boys. I know her well enough," he told his cousin, then added, "Call it a gut feeling."

Callum nodded and held up his hands. "Okay, cuz. Good enough for me."

Brady wasn't fooled by his cousin's tone for a moment. Because they were still at work, though, Brady felt it prudent not to comment on Callum's words of caution.

Instead, he went back to work.

Because he was still engaged in learning all the preliminary details involved in running the concierge desk, Brady wound up putting in an extra-long day.

He wasn't able to get back home until almost nine thirty.

As he let himself in, Brady couldn't help thinking back to when nine thirty was just the beginning of the evening for him, not the tail end of the day.

Now it felt like he had put in an eternity and a half since this morning. All he could think of was crawling into bed—fully dressed—and falling asleep.

As Brady turned the key in the lock, opening the front door, he fervently prayed that his human jumping beans had been put to bed. Even so, he had visions of them standing on the other side of the door, ready to jump up at him.

Ready to play.

With this unsettling image in mind, Brady slowly eased open the front door, looking around twice before finally stepping inside the house.

As he did so, he released the breath he was holding. It didn't seem possible, but the twins had to be asleep. Otherwise, he *knew* they would have come bounding out of nowhere to greet him.

Listening, Brady embraced what were clearly the sounds of silence, praying they would last until he could reach the sanctuary of his bedroom and shut the doors.

"Don't you want to eat?"

Surprised by the voice that seemed to come out of nowhere, Brady swung around and saw Harper standing a few feet away.

Once she saw Brady pull up outside, Harper had debated keeping silent and just letting him go up to his room before going home herself. Not only did she know he had to be tired, but that way they wouldn't have to finish the conversation they'd started that morning. She could put off having to explain why she hadn't been able to work as a nanny for months.

But doing that would mean allowing Brady to go to his room without having anything to eat. Of course, he might have very well gotten something to eat before he left the Hotel Fortune, but in good conscience, she didn't want to just assume things.

So, she put her own comfort aside and asked her question the moment he entered.

Brady didn't answer the question immediately. He just stared at Harper as her question finally registered.

Finally finding his tongue, Brady answered her. "Thanks, but after getting Team Chaos bedded down for the night, you probably just want to go home and get some well-earned rest yourself."

She had to admit that his answer caught her off guard. But then, she didn't think that way.

"I know I'm just the nanny, but I don't see my job ending when those little dynamite sticks defuse and close their big blue eyes," she informed him. "Besides, when you called earlier to say you'd be working late, I decided to make you a light dinner. I figured that anything heavy wouldn't sit well and might wind up keeping you awake." Harper gestured toward the kitchen. "Come," she invited. "Sit."

The tone was one he guessed that she used on the twins. "I'm not a little boy," he pointed out.

"No, you're not," she agreed. "But you don't have to be a little boy to need a little accommodating yourself. I'm just doing my part," she told him with a smile. "And the sooner you stop arguing with me and eat, the sooner we can both go to bed."

No sooner had she said that than the words replayed themselves in her head.

Appalled at how that had to have sounded, she turned a bright shade of red from her cheeks all the way to the tips of her ears.

Her eyes darted toward his face. "I mean—"

At another time, Brady might have gotten a kick out of watching Harper try to talk her way out of what she had inadvertently said. But he was tired and besides, he actually felt bad for her. After all, he reminded himself, the young woman was just being kind and thoughtful, going out of her way for him. Making her feel uncomfortable was no way to pay her back.

"I know what you mean, Harper, and you're right. I should just shut my mouth and stop giving you a hard time for being so thoughtful." He sat down at the table, all but collapsing in the chair. "Just know that if the meal involves a lot of chewing," Brady warned, "I'm not really up to it. I know my day was nothing like what you probably went through," he allowed, "but I feel as if someone used my body as a dust mop to clean everything up throughout the entire hotel."

Harper looked at him, genuinely concerned and sympathetic.

"I did not have a day anything like that," she

told him. "Actually, the boys and I had a great deal of fun today. I admit that they do require a lot of energy to keep up with," she qualified. "But they *did* listen to me, which I consider an extremely important part of the whole."

Brady couldn't help thinking of all the other nannies who had come, and then gone, through his doors. The ones who threw their hands up just before they walked out and the ones who had rather sharp, painful things to say about the twins' attitude before they, too, left.

For the umpteenth time, Brady thought of how very lucky he was to have stumbled across this saint of a woman.

Which brought him back to the question he had had for her this morning. What had made her leave her last place of employment without having another place waiting as backup?

But just as he was about to ask, Harper placed a large, steaming bowl of chicken noodle soup on the table before him.

The aroma was exceedingly tempting.

So much so that it succeeded in enticing him and suddenly, Brady realized that he was incredibly hungry and could most definitely eat.

But before he did, he raised a quizzical eyebrow in Harper's direction.

Harper put her own interpretation to the expression on his face. He wanted to know why she was serving him this rather than a sandwich or a piece of chicken.

"I figured that you might welcome some comfort food at this point," she explained. "The most comforting thing I could think of was chicken soup."

Brady laughed softly as he picked up his spoon. "So now you're a mind reader."

"It comes with the territory. It's a basic requirement when you're a nanny." She said that with such a straight face, for a moment he thought Harper was serious.

Brady waited for the first spoonful to wind its way through his body. She was right. It *was* comforting. "Well, in my book, you're an angel."

She shook her head. "Uh-uh."

She was rejecting something he clearly meant as a compliment. Curious, he asked, "Why not?"

"The wings would make it really hard to get through doorways," she explained. "It would also make it hard to chase after mischievous little boys."

"I am way too tired to argue," Brady told her. Although not too tired, he thought, to respond to the smile that curved her lips.

"Good," she declared.

Yes, *it was*, Brady thought. But the assessment really had nothing to do with her being an angel.

Chapter Eleven

There was no doubt about it. Brady found himself torn when it came to Harper.

Part of him was utterly thrilled that he had, through no real efforts of his own, found her and hired her to be the twins' nanny. The woman was clearly perfect for the job.

But at the same time, there was a part of him that regretted hiring her because being her employer tied his hands. He couldn't make any sort of a romantic move on her because that would ruin everything. Not to mention that it would put both of them in an awkward position.

But despite that, something told him that Harper Radcliffe could very possibly be "the one." The one who could, quite simply, complete him.

They hadn't even kissed and yet he felt that there were some definite vibes there. Vibes that told him, given half a chance, he and Harper could have something very special.

Get a grip, man, Brady ordered himself, his mind straying from his work. *Look at what you have and not what you "might" have.*

As the boys' nanny, Harper brought him incredible peace of mind and as far as Brady was concerned, peace of mind was worth more than gold.

He needed to keep his thoughts from drifting and daydreaming. Right now he had a real problem to deal with. One that, as the days went by and he got more and more of a handle on his job at the hotel, grew more serious in nature. His family had told him that two months ago, there had been an incident at the hotel—a serious one.

According to what Callum had said, the balcony had seemed to suddenly give way. The whole thing could have turned out to be a lot worse than it was, but bad enough that there had been even one person on that balcony when it had given out. He supposed they'd gotten lucky, considering that the so-called accident had occurred during a Fortune family gathering. Grace Williams, the first hospitality trainee to be hired at the hotel, was the person who was injured. She had hurt her ankle and was on the mend, thankfully. She was now working as the hotel's manager and was also engaged to Brady's cousin Wiley.

Still, any way Brady looked at it, it was an injury that should not have happened. Closer inspection of the balcony had uncovered that the incident might not have been an accident. It seemed possible that the balcony beams had been tampered with.

If that was true, it would mean someone was attempting to sabotage what Callum and his brothers were trying to build.

So far, Callum told Brady when he first filled him in about the incident, the police hadn't been able to find proof one way or another. But Kane had reviewed the damage—and his inspection certificates received prior to the accident—and he was almost positive that the break had been caused deliberately. Which meant that until that culprit was found and brought to justice, the general feeling among the Fortunes was that they had to keep an eye out around the hotel.

Brady kept it low-key and never spoke about it in front of the guests, but he encountered one of the management interns in the back office days later.

"So how's the investigation progressing?" he

asked Jay Cross point-blank one afternoon when he ran into the trainee. It struck him that Jay had that cowboy look about him, as if he had just come in from riding his favorite horse, instead of conducting business at the hotel.

The dark-haired man knew immediately what Brady was referring to. "No hard and fast suspects yet," Jay responded. "At least, no suspicions that panned out yet," he amended, "but everyone here has been on the lookout for any unusual behavior that might point us toward the right suspect. Or at least in the right direction," he qualified. "Eventually, though, the perpetrator will make some sort of a misstep that'll give him or her away. Whoever did this can't get away with it forever," Jay maintained with conviction.

But Brady didn't feel as confident as Jay did. "You really believe that?"

"Absolutely," Jay replied without any hesitation. "Everyone makes mistakes and that's what eventually gives them away. If he or she is sloppy, it'll be soon. If they turn out *not* to be sloppy, it'll probably take longer to find them. But it *will* happen," Jay said with certainty. "It's just a matter of time. Until then, take heart in the fact that we'll *all* be on the lookout."

Brady merely nodded and wound up paying lip service to what had been meant as words of comfort.

Well, Brady thought as he drove home that evening, the job was definitely not without its challenges. And heaven knew it certainly wasn't dull. But he was not about to complain. He got to work with a lot of different people and focus on keeping the hotel running smoothly. Plus, of course there was that mystery to solve.

Brady was well aware of how the public's mind worked. If the Hotel Fortune suddenly attained the reputation that it wasn't safe, no one would want to stay or dine there, and business would go from a growing enterprise to a non-existent one.

They needed to catch whoever had done this. And soon.

A thought suddenly hit Brady. Maybe it was someone with a vendetta against the Fortune family in general, or perhaps just one Fortune family member in particular.

What they needed, he thought, was to take a closer look at just who might profit if the hotel was suddenly failing.

He had a great deal to occupy his mind, Brady thought as he pulled up to his house.

Including Harper.

Her world revolved around Toby and Tyler now. But that definitely didn't mean that her work was any less challenging than his. It was just on an entirely different level.

And, Brady thought, Harper didn't even have any adults to talk to during the day in order to help maintain her sanity. That had to be more than a little challenging for her.

The least he could do, he decided, was to attempt to bolster her.

Standing on his doorstep, Brady pulled back his shoulders and pasted a smile on his lips before opening the door and walking in.

The first thing that registered was the toys scattered everywhere. Toys he had initially bought for the twins in an effort to keep them occupied. That never succeeded for more than a few minutes. Maybe a couple of hours, tops. But in the end, the toys just contributed to the overall feeling of chaos.

Right now it felt as if he had just walked in on the aftermath of a war.

"Who won?" he heard himself asking Harper, who was on the floor, tossing toys into a huge box meant to house them and keep them from being underfoot.

Surprised, she looked up at Brady. Doing her best to tidy up, or at least gather up as many toys as she could, Harper had managed to lose track of time. She hadn't thought that Brady would be home yet.

Obviously she had miscalculated.

"That hasn't been determined yet," Harper

admitted. "But I was ultimately hoping it would turn out to be a draw."

"You're too modest. My money's on you," Brady told her, picking up a toy truck that had managed to lose one of its rear wheels. He tossed the truck into the large collection box.

"Optimist," she said with a laugh. Harper nodded at the remaining toys—they still comprised a large heap. "Why don't you just leave all that?" she suggested. "You've put in a long day. You shouldn't have to come home and spend more time cleaning up after the twins."

She was referring to his work at the hotel, Brady thought, trying to remember if he had shared anything with her or if that was just her natural ability to intuit things.

"The way I see it, Harper," he told her, continuing to gather the toys off the floor, "you put in a long day, too."

Rather than grumbling, the way some of the other nannies before her had done in situations far less trying, Brady watched as a smile blossomed over Harper's appealing face.

"Yes, but my day consisted of playing games and teaching Toby and Tyler how to be patient while the other twin had his turn at one of those games. By the way, Tyler has a real aptitude at board games while Toby has excellent hand-eye coordination when it comes to video games," she told him.

Brady remembered the last time he had played a video game with them. He had wound up breaking the twins apart when the game went up to a higher level.

Laughing, he shook his head. "No doubt about it. I don't care what you say—you're clearly a saint."

He was embarrassing her. "You're exaggerating way too much."

But he had another perspective. "If anything, I'm understating things," Brady told her.

She made her way over on her knees to another pile of toys. "You know, you don't have to flatter me. I've already told you that I'm staying."

Brady grinned as he followed her, picking up toys along with her. "Call it insurance. And I really did mean what I said. No flattery intended," he told her. "Until you came along, I saw grown women break down in tears or go running out the door, threatening me with bills from their psychiatrists as they ran."

Harper shook her head. "If a woman is that fragile, she has no business trying to help raise overactive children."

Trying his best to be fair, Brady emphasized the full picture. "Hey, there's two of them to do the damage. Sometimes the nanny felt outnumbered." He found himself moving closer toward Harper as the pile of toys grew smaller and more manageable. "So, what wonderful things did they do today? Or am I safer not knowing?" he asked.

Harper got a kick out of the way Brady had worded his question—and the way out he had given her. Her grin widened. "Let's just say that what you don't know won't hurt you."

There seemed something almost ominous about the way she put that, Brady thought. She had piqued his curiosity.

"Does that ever end well?" he wanted to know, rolling her words over in his mind.

"It's just better if we leave it at that. Trust me," she added as she bent down to pick up yet another toy that had seen better days.

"Guess I'll just have to," Brady agreed as he bent down to pick up the same toy.

They managed to bump foreheads and as they raised their heads up at the same time, they wound up having their faces almost perfectly aligned.

Which also meant that their lips were inches apart.

All the pep talks he had given himself, all the reasons he had laid out as to why he couldn't allow his feelings to get the better of him, all that went up in smoke.

Before he knew it, he let his instincts take

over and the next moment, Brady found himself kissing her.

The fallen toy was completely forgotten as it toppled back down to the floor. Instead of a broken truck, Brady was holding on to Harper's shoulders. Rising to his feet, his lips on hers, he brought her up with him.

The kiss continued and as it did, it generated a lot of warm, vibrant feelings that went coursing through Harper, taking her very breath away.

More than anything, she was tempted to go with it, to follow this feeling wherever it might take her.

But she knew she couldn't.

The twins were what was important here, not her feelings or her very strong attraction to Brady. She had already been forewarned that this road would lead to nowhere.

Reluctantly she drew her head back just an inch. "Um, I've got dinner on the stove warming for you," she said.

That wasn't the only thing she had warming, Brady couldn't help thinking, more than a little tempted to steal just another second longer with this incredibly arousing woman.

"Does Unca Brady have a boo-boo?"

They all but jumped apart at the sound of the small voice asking the question. Brady and Harper turned toward the voice, almost in unison, to see Tyler standing in the living room doorway. He appeared to be rubbing sleep from his eye.

Harper, Brady noted, turned out to be extremely quick on her feet. Recovering her composure, she asked the little boy, "What makes you ask that, Tyler?"

"'Cause when I fell and hurt my knee, you kissed my boo-boo to make it all better," Tyler reminded Harper. "Did you fall on your face, Unca Brady?" the little boy wanted to know. His voice echoed with sympathy.

Relieved to have an answer for him, Brady went with the excuse the little boy had all but handed him on a silver platter. "Yes, that's it, Tyler. I tripped and fell on my face."

Tyler looked Brady over very carefully. Brady waited for the twin to point out that there were no marks anywhere on his face. Instead, the boy merely nodded.

"Harper made it all better, didn't she?" he asked his guardian. "Just like my mama used to," the little boy added wistfully.

Brady's heart filled up, and he found himself at a loss for words. Instead, he put his hand on the boy's shoulder, giving it a quick squeeze.

Tyler's words definitely tugged on Harper's heart as well. Whatever might have happened between her and Brady was pushed into the background, officially bringing that part of the evening to a close as far as she was concerned.

"Tyler, would you like to help me get your uncle Brady's dinner for him?" she asked the boy.

Tyler surprised both of them by asking, "Will that help his boo-boo go away?"

"Oh definitely," Harper assured the boy, glancing in Brady's direction for backup.

"Nothing would make me feel better faster than getting something to eat," Brady said, playing along with the game.

The boy's small head bobbed up and down, the question of helping out obviously settled.

"Sure I'll help," he told Harper, then added solemnly, "I want him to feel better. I don't want anything to happen to Unca Brady." He turned around to look at Brady, his small face extremely serious. "Be careful, Unca Brady. Don't hurt your face," the little boy warned him.

"I'll be careful," Brady assured the twin.

But Tyler still looked very skeptical. "Do you promise?" he asked his guardian.

Surprised that Tyler cared that much, Brady told him, "I promise."

But Tyler still wouldn't let him off the hook. "Cross your heart?"

Harper could see that Brady was struggling

not to laugh. Mentally, she kept her fingers crossed.

"My heart, my eyes, and anything else you want crossed," Brady told the boy.

Getting the answer he wanted, Tyler burst into giggles, his solemn expression a thing of the past. "Okay!"

"Well, if the negotiations are over," Harper told the twin, "then I'm still going to need your help in the kitchen, Tyler."

Determined to please, Tyler's small brow furrowed up. "What's nego-nego—that word?" he wanted to know.

Tyler definitely was a sponge when it came to soaking up knowledge, Harper thought. "Negotiations," she repeated. "Why don't I explain it while you help me?" She took his hand and led him into the kitchen, patiently answering his questions on the way.

As he went to help his nanny warm up dinner, Tyler looked as if he could levitate right where he walked.

Looking at Harper, Brady knew the feeling.

Chapter Twelve

The more he saw her in action, the more Brady found himself to be totally in awe of Harper. She was nothing short of phenomenal when it came to handling the twins.

As much as Brady hated to admit it—because he had once seen himself as being able to master any and every situation he came across—when it came to parenting and disciplining two rambunctious little boys, Brady was totally out of his league.

Even after putting in six grueling months on the job, he still didn't have the vaguest idea what to do when it came to managing the twins.

He just wasn't cut out for parenting, Brady thought, resigned. While Harper seemed to be a natural. Somehow, she just instinctively knew what to do, how to get the lively twins to back off. And, more important, how to get them to behave.

Moreover, she could get them to *want* to behave.

It seemed to Brady that the two hellions who had come roaring into his life on an express train were in competition with one another as to who could be the more well-behaved around Harper. And, he'd noticed, in competition as to who could manage to earn her first smile of the day.

"You don't drug them, do you?"

Harper looked at Brady, stunned by his question and certain she had to have misheard what he had just said. "Excuse me?"

"I'm joking." He held up his hands and grinned. "But I am curious. They're…well, not exactly calm," he said tactfully, "but less wild around you than they are around me. Why is that?"

She smiled at him. The man certainly needed to be educated in the ways of children and their instincts. "Because they sense they can have their way with you while they're not that sure how far they can push me. And, I'm happy to say, I get the feeling that they don't want to do something that might make me leave."

It was the tail end of another excruciatingly long day. Brady had come home early—and had come very close to regretting it. His intention had been to attempt to bond with the boys, but that just wasn't happening. After much bargaining—and with Harper coming in to back him up—he had succeeded in getting the twins to bed.

When he had followed her out of the boys' room and made his way downstairs, he was completely wiped out. "Let's face it," Brady told Harper when she had asked him if there was anything wrong, "I'm just not cut out for this."

"This?" Harper questioned, clearing away the last of the mess that the twins had managed to create as they played today.

"Being a parent," Brady answered, then specified, "Child-rearing." He took in a disheartened, shaky breath as he added, "While you, you're a natural. I'm surprised that you don't have kids of your own," he told her.

"It takes the right man for that," she answered. Their eyes met for a long moment, communicating things neither was free to say out loud yet. But it was still there.

Clearing her throat, she turned her attention to what Brady had said previously. Sitting down on the sofa, she patted the place beside her, silently urging Brady to take a seat.

"That's a very nice compliment you gave me earlier," she told him as he sat down beside her. "But not a very realistic one. Nobody starts out knowing what to do when it comes to kids. I've been working as a nanny for several years now because I love kids, but I certainly didn't come on the scene knowing what to do. I had to learn that just the way that everyone else did. Just like you," she emphasized, deliberately looking into his eyes as she made her point.

"I haven't learned anything and it's been over six months," Brady protested.

He was selling himself short, Harper thought. "Six months of you adjusting to the situation you found yourself thrown into, headfirst," she declared. "Six months of you adjusting to the needs of two mischievous, overactive, demanding little boys while learning how to put your own needs a distant second." Didn't he realize that, she wondered.

"If you ask me, all things considered, I think that you're doing very well, Brady. Give yourself a break and a little credit here," she urged him, placing her hand over his.

Then suddenly realizing what she was doing, Harper pulled back her hand. But she didn't withdraw her seal of approval, which was evident in what she said to him. "If you ask me, Brady, you're being much too hard on yourself."

Brady frowned, shaking his head. "I don't know about that," he said.

"Well, I do," she informed him with certainty. "The thing that you have to remember is the most important requirement of being a parent—or a guardian," she emphasized. "A heart."

He laughed dryly. "I'm pretty sure my doctor said I had one on my last checkup."

"I'm serious, wise guy," Harper chided with a laugh. "If you truly care about them—and trust me, kids have a way of sensing if you do or don't—then everything else will just fall into place. And, the way I see it, you have enough love for both of us." Harper's words played themselves back in her head the moment she said them. She instantly turned crimson. "I mean—"

The woman had just spent several minutes trying to make him feel better about himself as a surrogate parent. He wasn't about to have her struggling to walk back something she'd had no intention of saying in the first place.

"I know what you mean," Brady assured her. "And I do appreciate it."

For a moment, he debated asking the question that had resurfaced in his mind, the one he had asked her days ago. Ordinarily, he would just let it go. But the more he got to know her, the more curious he found himself about the details of her life.

"You know," he said, approaching the question cautiously, "you never did tell me why you decided to leave your last position."

As he watched, the confident, outgoing young woman, who was such a natural when it came to handling the two free-spirited boys he had taken into his home, suddenly became introverted and reticent.

After a long beat, Harper finally said, "My last job didn't end well," growing more uncomfortable with each word she uttered.

But she could see that Brady was waiting for more information. She forced herself to say something, while still keeping it as vague as possible. Because although she liked him and was coming to think of Brady as a fair man, ultimately she didn't know how he would react to the reason she had been fired. After all, it was just her word against her former employer's. What if he didn't believe her? At the very least, that would bother her. At its worst, it might cause Brady to fire her. She decided not to go into it.

Since it happened, she had done her best not to think about the circumstances at all. But it wasn't easy. "Let's just say that the situation became... complicated," she finally told him.

"Complicated?" Brady questioned.

"Complicated," she repeated, saying the word with such finality that he knew the subject was closed until further notice.

Possibly permanently.

In any event, Brady knew when to back away and not push the situation.

Switching directions, Brady didn't entirely drop the subject, just decided to approach it from another angle.

"I think the reason you're so good at what you do is because you become emotionally involved with your charges and their families." He sighed. That wasn't anything that he could have been able to deal with. "It comes naturally to you," he said. "Me, not so much," he admitted. "As a matter of fact, I can't say that I'm really any good at something like that."

Something like that.

Was he telling her that he wasn't one to get emotionally involved—or worse, was he warning her off? She didn't know, but in any case, she wasn't about to buy any trouble. It might do her good to keep a distance between herself and this sexy, good-looking man.

A man she had already kissed and would have gone on kissing—or more—had Tyler not had a bad dream and come downstairs looking for her and interrupted them.

The fact that Brady had also kissed her back—

and maybe had even been the one to initiate the kiss—wasn't really that important. What was important was that they *had* kissed and that kiss could have very well blossomed into something a great deal more if not for Tyler's untimely entrance.

She was going to have to keep her guard up against that sort of thing ever repeating itself.

That would bring a whole new meaning to the word *complicated*, she thought.

It was definitely time to retreat, she thought. Gathering herself together, Harper suddenly rose to her feet. "Let me get you dinner," she told him with forced cheerfulness.

Brady caught hold of her hand to stop her. Abruptly realizing what he was doing, he released her hand. When she looked at him quizzically, he told her, "I didn't hire you to serve me meals, Harper. I hired you to be Toby and Tyler's nanny."

"I know that," she answered crisply. "But it doesn't hurt to go the extra mile and make an extra serving when cooking for the boys and myself. Unless you don't like my cooking," she suddenly realized. Was that why he was saying no? Because he didn't like what she made?

"Anything I don't have to cook myself tastes great," he told her, then assured her with feeling,

"But so far, everything you've made has been really exceptionally delicious."

Harper grinned. "Nice save," she congratulated Brady.

"Not bad for a man who's half asleep," Brady conceded with a tired smile.

Harper laughed warmly at his comment, her revived sense of humor bringing her old self back to the foreground. With a wink, she told Brady, "Not even bad for a man who's wide awake. Come, follow me," she urged, leading the way.

Brady's stomach grumbled as he followed Harper to the kitchen. The grumbling reminded him that he had completely lost track of the last time that he had actually eaten today.

Harper was more than happy to turn her attention toward doing something productive instead of wrestling with her growing feelings and digging up situations that made her feel very uncomfortable. Her last job was in the past and she fully intended to keep it there rather than to draw it out and expose it to the light of day.

Heaven knew it wasn't because she had ever harbored even the slightest feelings for her last employer's husband. On the contrary, by the time she had been given her walking papers, Edward Wheeler had made her skin crawl with his very presence. The idea of anything happening between them was enough to make her physically ill. The man had turned out to be a notorious player and it galled Harper that his wife actually believed that she would do anything so reprehensible as to have a romantic affair with the father of the children she was being paid to watch over and take care of.

That would have been a terrible breach of trust on her part and she just wasn't that type of person. It hurt her that the woman would even *think* that was possible.

Water under the bridge, Harper silently insisted.

No, the subject was better left closed and under wraps, Harper thought. If she said anything about it to Brady, gave him any sort of details, then at some point, she was certain the subject would resurface again and haunt her.

That was the last thing she wanted, Harper thought. She had a new job, back doing what she loved, and she wasn't about to risk that because of something that never happened.

Harper roused herself, bringing her mind back to the present. Placing a serving of pork chops, mashed potatoes and green beans in front of Brady, she told him, "If there's nothing else, I think I'll be going home now. The boys were particularly active today and to be honest, my batteries are drained and need recharging," she confessed.

"You didn't even have to do this," Brady reminded her. "All I need from you is to take care of the boys. That was what we had agreed on at the outset," he reminded her. "I could have found something to eat."

"And mess up the kitchen while you were doing it?" she asked. She had seen Brady when he was searching for something. The man was definitely *not* neat. He was more like a tornado that had been let loose. "No, this way's better," Harper assured him. "Less to clean up in the long run."

Unable to resist, he cut a piece of pork chop and slipped it into his mouth. For a second, the expression on his face looked like that of a man who had unexpectedly found his way into heaven. "This is really good," he told her with feeling.

Pleased, Harper smiled with satisfaction. "Toby and Tyler thought so, too."

Moved, he couldn't let this pass without telling her how valuable she had become to his life in such a short amount of time. "I am so glad you're here, Harper."

That caught her off guard. *He didn't mean that the way it sounded*, she warned herself. He was just talking about her cooking and how she managed the boys.

Not wanting him to think she was rude,

Harper told him, "I'm glad to be here, too," as she began to make her way out of the kitchen.

"No, you don't understand," Brady said. "Until you got here, dinner used to consist of hot dogs, hamburgers and the occasional pizza." He knew there was no excuse for that, but sometimes easy was better than nothing at all. "Until you came into their lives, Toby and Tyler didn't realize that vegetables could actually be a tasty part of an evening meal."

He had such an adorable expression on his face, Harper couldn't help laughing. "Then I'm glad I came along," she told him. "I guess that would explain why the twins thought soda pop was one of the essential food groups," she teased.

"Like I said," Brady told her after taking another healthy-sized bite of the seasoned pork chop, "I make a terrible parent."

She was not about to stand for him putting himself down. "The most important part of being a parent is wanting to be there—and you were. You *are*," Harper emphasized, her eyes meeting his. "Now, if there's nothing else," she told him, "I'll be leaving."

There *was* something else. He wanted to ask her just to stay at the table and keep him company. Nothing more than that.

But at the same time, he knew that was being selfish. Harper had certainly earned her rest and the least he could do was let her go home and get to bed.

The word *bed* instantly conjured up images in his mind that had absolutely no business being there. Images of Harper sprawled across his king-size bed, her arms stretched out to him as he lowered himself over her.

All the more reason to send her on her way, he thought. Heaven knew that if he had her stay, that would tempt him to want to progress to something more than just conversation, and if he went that route, he risked having her leave.

Permanently.

He had already risked losing her with that juvenile stunt he had pulled that day while she had been picking up toys and he had gone to help her—and wound up doing something completely out of character, Brady upbraided himself. If it hadn't been for Tyler and his nightmare, who knew what might have happened?

He couldn't allow that to happen a second time no matter how attractive he found Harper, Brady thought. Without knowing it, that little boy had managed to rescue the situation—and him. Because, if Harper hadn't miraculously come into his life, who knew where he and the boys would be right now? Or, for that matter, if he could even manage to juggle work and this situation he had somehow found himself in.

"Sorry. I didn't mean to keep you," Brady apologized. "Go home, get some well-deserved rest so that you can put your track shoes on in the morning and keep up with those little whirling dervishes."

His words created an image in her head and Harper couldn't help but laugh.

"That is a very colorful way to describe them," Harper told him with approval.

"Really? I thought I was actually understating the situation. Heaven knew that until you came along, I felt like someone trapped inside of a never-ending cartoon program."

Harper smiled as she made it to the front door and opened it. "Glad I could change that for you," she told Brady.

Brady watched as she walked out of the house.

"Yeah," he murmured under his breath to her back. "Me, too."

Chapter Thirteen

Things were progressing well at the Hotel Fortune and even his home life had seemed to fall
into some sort of a heartening routine, Brady
thought. While he couldn't exactly say that
things had become peaceful, at least they were
no longer in a state of constant turmoil.

If there was a fly in the ointment, it was that
the search for the person who was behind that
balcony collapse had not been fruitful. The investigation was ongoing and while some of the
suspects had been cleared, there were still a lot
of people who needed to be investigated.

Brady found that really frustrating and dis-
turbing.

In an effort to keep moving forward and remain productive, Brady forced himself to focus on the positive things and not obsess over the negative.

Easier said than done, he thought late one evening after Harper had gone home and he was in bed. He found his thoughts turning toward her and that really didn't help him, either. During the day, when his time was filled to the brim with hotel concerns, it was easy not to think about Harper. And even when he came home and the twins were still bouncing around, all he could concentrate on was how much his life had changed.

But once they had been put to bed, Harper left and the house grew quiet, it was really hard for him not to think about her and how she had brought such incredible order and peace of mind into his life.

And by the same token—even after she went home for the night—how she also managed to fire up his imagination and stir his longing.

Really stir his longing.

No woman had ever been front and center in his life. That wasn't to say that he didn't enjoy their company whenever he could, but he had never been singularly focused on any of these women.

However, it seemed that lately, totally unbidden, Harper kept popping up in his thoughts as well as occasionally in his dreams. He kept telling himself he shouldn't—couldn't—allow any of these mental meanderings to bear fruit. And yet, no matter what he did, he couldn't seem to eliminate the really powerful longing he felt for her.

Any way he looked at it, it was an explosion waiting to happen.

Brady had shared a particularly nice evening meal with her tonight as well as an extended conversation centering around the twins'—mainly Toby's—exploits at preschool. But when he and Harper parted company, it was her smile, not the conversation or even the really tasty meal she had prepared, that insisted on lingering on his mind.

And was now keeping him awake.

He couldn't keep doing this to himself, Brady silently insisted, turning on his other side and punching his pillow in an attempt to get it into a comfortable, more welcoming shape.

He wasn't succeeding.

So when the phone rang after ten o'clock that night, he was still awake and up to answering it. Hoping this didn't involve some sort of an unforeseen hotel emergency, Brady mentally crossed his fingers and picked up his cell.

Braced for anything, he said, "Hello?"

"Hi, Big Brother, how's it going?"

At the sound of the cheerful, soprano voice in his ear, Brady immediately bolted upright in bed and propped himself up against the headboard.

"Arabella?" he asked although he was certain that it had to be her.

He hadn't heard from his only sister in a while now. Because it was Arabella, he just assumed that she was too busy having fun to bother calling. She had a zest for life he almost envied now. The next moment, he realized that he wouldn't change anything about the way his life had evolved, chaos and all. He admitted to himself that he had grown to care about the twins. When had that happened, he marveled.

"You have any other sisters I don't know about?" Arabella asked him, amused.

"No, in your case one is definitely enough," he assured her. And then he grew a little more serious. "Is anything wrong? Are Mom and Dad okay?" he wanted to know.

Brady was aware that his sister, four years his junior and incredibly independent in her dealings, kept unorthodox hours. However, since he had become the twins' guardian, he looked at things in a far different light than he had back when his days had been carefree and life hadn't been nearly as structured as it was now.

Now he was more aware of the darker things

in life and the consequences they could bring with them.

"They're fine, Brady. Does something have to be wrong for me to call my favorite big brother?" his sister asked.

Uh-oh, he thought, the phrase *favorite big brother* setting off alarms.

"No," Brady answered, "but you have to admit, Belle, you don't usually call. So what's up?" he wanted to know.

"Maybe I've just decided that it's time for me to grow up a little," Arabella answered—a bit too loftily in his opinion.

"Are you sure there's nothing wrong?" Brady asked again. Because of the chaos the twins had initially brought into his life, he wasn't about to take things at face value anymore and coast. He liked being prepared for possible disasters *before* they happened.

"Yes, I'm sure," Arabella answered. "Relax, Brady. I just wanted to see how you and your little wild bunch were doing—although I have to admit, until you turned this into an interrogation, you did sound as if you're more relaxed than you were the last time we talked." She laughed as an image came to mind. "For instance, you don't sound as if you're in the middle of fighting an out-of-control five-alarm fire."

"That's because I'm not," he told her. Since

she had expressed an interest, he decided to fill her in. "Things are going pretty well with my new job—and as for the *wild bunch* as you called them, they're actually beginning to calm down—at least enough for me to be able to catch my breath."

"What happened?" she wanted to know. "Did you find a doctor to write a prescription for junior-sized tranquilizers?" Arabella teased.

He was more than happy to give credit where credit was due. "Even better. I found a nanny who's absolutely incredible. Her name's Harper Radcliffe," he told his sister before she could ask. "And she's really fantastic with the twins," he added with wholehearted enthusiasm.

His passionate tone was not lost on his sister. "Is that all she's great with?" Arabella asked, amusement evident in her voice.

Alarms went off in Brady's head. "Hey, you're reading much too much into this, Belle." He laughed shortly. "I see you're still a hopeless romantic."

"Not hopeless," Arabella protested, wanting to set her brother straight.

He noticed that she hadn't vetoed his entire statement. "But you are a romantic," he countered.

Arabella sniffed. "Not everything has to be labeled, Big Brother," she told him. Before he could argue the point, she got back to the reason she had called. "So then you feel that everything is going well in Rambling Rose?" she pressed. "You don't have any regrets about moving there?"

"No, not for one minute," Brady readily assured his sister.

"Well, that's good to hear." She paused for a moment, then decided to release her bombshell. Like ripping off a Band-Aid, she decided to do it quickly. "Especially since I've been thinking of making the move to your fair town myself."

The thought of seeing his sister again pleased him. In his estimation, it had already been far too long. The last time they had seen one another, he was still living in upstate New York. "Really?"

"Really," Arabella replied, pleasure throbbing in her voice.

And then she hesitated, just for a moment, as she gathered her courage together. If he said no to this, it would turn out to be very awkward.

"If I did come out, would you be able to put me up until I found a place of my own? Or would I be in the way?" she quickly asked.

Arabella wanted everything out in the open and if her brother, despite his protest, had something going with this "fantastic" nanny of his, the last thing she wanted to do was interfere with that. She didn't want him resenting her presence.

Brady knew exactly what his sister was driving at and he immediately put an end to that line of thinking.

"No, you wouldn't be in the way," he told Arabella. "But for your own sake, you might want to rethink staying here."

She didn't understand. If he didn't think she would be getting in the way, why would she want to rethink staying with him? It didn't make any sense to her.

Arabella put the question to him. "Why?"

Brady didn't mince any words. "Do you think you're up to putting up with the boys twenty-four/seven?" he wanted to know.

She didn't hesitate. "Sure. I haven't seen them since before you moved to Rambling Rose. They've probably grown at least six inches. Maybe even a foot," she teased.

"Not quite," he answered. "Okay, then consider yourself invited to stay," he told her. "Just let me know when you're going to be coming out."

"Will do," Arabella promised. And then she circled around to the *real* reason that she had called him. "So, things are going well for you at the hotel?" she asked again, searching for a way to broach the question that was foremost on her mind.

"For the most part, yes," he answered. He was becoming suspicious now. "Why do you ask?"

"Oh, no reason," she said quickly. "I just want to know if you're happy. Oh, by the way," Arabella began a little too innocently, "did you happen to run into Jay Cross anywhere while you've been working at the hotel?"

At the mention of the man's name, Brady's mind went back to the discussion he'd had with Jay regarding the ongoing investigation into the balcony incident.

"I think I talked to him about a week ago," he told his sister. Then, because he had a feeling that this was what she was ultimately getting at, he told Arabella, "He's doing well there."

Pausing, Brady didn't hear his sister say anything in response, so he decided to press her. "Why do you want to know?"

"No reason, really," she answered a little too quickly and too innocently. Realizing that her brother probably wasn't fooled and wasn't about to let the matter drop unless she gave him some sort of an actual reason for her question, Arabella cast about and managed to come up with something. "Jay was nice to me when we met at Larkin's birthday party back in January," she said, mentioning their little nephew, "and I was just wondering if he was still in town, that's all."

She wasn't fooling him for a second. Arabella

was displaying too much interest in Jay Cross. But for the time being, Brady decided to play along. "Yes, he's still there."

Hearing his tone, Arabella frowned. "Get rid of that smirk in your voice, Big Brother."

"I don't know what you're talking about," he said a bit too quickly.

"Yeah, right." She laughed at him. "You never did learn how to lie well."

"We can't all be as convincing when it comes to fabricating things as you are, Belle," he told her. And then he dropped his bantering tone. "It'll be great to see you again, Belle."

"You sure you don't mind fitting me in?" she questioned, somewhat serious now. "Between your job and your nanny, you must be awfully busy."

Brady heard only one thing in the question she posed. She was making assumptions and he intended to set his sister straight immediately.

"She's not 'my' nanny, Belle," he told her seriously. "She's Toby and Tyler's nanny."

"Right." Arabella couldn't keep the smile from her face. "I'll try to remember that. Okay, I'll let you get back to your beauty sleep. And I'll give you a call just before I'm ready to move to your neck of the woods," she told him.

Brady laughed, getting a kick out of his sister's phraseology. "Oh, you're going to fit right in here," he teased.

"I'll have you know that I fit in anywhere I set my mind to," Arabella informed him.

"I never doubted that," Brady replied. Lack of confidence had never been Arabella's problem.

He was still smiling to himself as he hung up. It seemed that little by little, his family was all relocating to this not-quite-so-dusty little town.

And he, for one, was really looking forward to seeing Belle here.

"C'mon, let's go!" Toby cried, eager to get Harper and his "unca" Brady out of the house. He was all set to make a mad dash for the car. "You're too slow," Toby complained, looking accusingly at his twin who was hanging back. Toby was shifting from foot to foot.

"I'm waiting for Unca Brady," Tyler told his twin, looking at his uncle loyally.

Harper had come in early carrying a packed picnic basket. She had promised the twins they would all go on a picnic on Saturday if they managed to be good for three days running.

As far as the twins were concerned, they had fulfilled their part of the bargain. As an added bonus, the twins had gotten Brady to agree to come along with them on this venture.

Harper looked at Brady dubiously now. "Are

you sure you want to come?" she asked as she allowed Toby to pull her out the front door.

"Are you trying to talk me out of it?" Brady asked, amused.

"No, heaven forbid. It's just that with all the hours you put in working at the hotel, it occurred to me that you don't get much time to rest," Harper explained.

Humor curved Brady's mouth as Tyler pulled on his arm, getting him closer to Harper's car. "Are you trying to say this little excursion won't be restful?" Brady asked innocently.

"Only if you compare this to being a lion tamer," Harper pointed out.

"That sounds intriguing," Brady said with a laugh.

Spurred on and inspired, Toby immediately began to make lion noises—or what the little boy thought passed for lion noises.

With the picnic basket already in the trunk, Harper placed a hand on either boy's shoulder and herded them both into the backseat of her vehicle where their car seats were waiting.

"Down, Simba," she told Toby.

Toby's brow furrowed as she secured the car seat straps. "Who's Simba?" he wanted to know.

She turned her attention to Tyler's straps. "That's a lion in a story," she told Toby.

"Do you know him?" both boys asked almost simultaneously.

"Not personally," she told the boys with a straight face.

"Nobody knows lions," Toby declared knowingly as he spoke up.

Tyler, however, would have believed Harper if she had told him she could walk on water. Backward.

"Harper does," he told his twin, then turned toward her for confirmation. "Right, Harper?"

"Not this time," she told Tyler. It was all she could do not to hug the boy. His innocence touched her heart. "Now let's go. My guess is that you don't want to miss this picnic, so we need to hurry."

The forecast was for rain later in the day and she'd already warned the boys that once the raindrops began to fall, they were out of there, no arguments. The twins had reluctantly agreed.

"You sure you don't want me to drive?" Brady asked her as she crawled out of the backseat and opened the driver's-side door.

"I'm sure." Her tone left no room for arguing. "This is your day off, remember?" she reminded him.

"When do you get a day off?" Brady wanted to know. So far, she seemed to have come in every day without fail.

She flashed him a wide grin. "What makes you think I'm working?" she deadpanned.

"Just kind of looked that way, that's all," Brady answered with a smile.

"When you love what you do, it's not work. You just sit back and relax," she told him, getting in and buckling up. "I'll handle the driving."

He looked a little dubious about the whole venture and then shrugged. "Sure, why not? My insurance is all paid up," he said as he got into the passenger seat, then buckled up.

She gave him a look that might or might not have been meant to put him in his place. "I'll ignore that," she said, starting up her car.

Brady braced himself against the dashboard. He'd never liked not being in control of the vehicle he was in.

As it turned out, though, he had nothing to worry about. But then, he told himself as they reached their destination, he should have known that.

Not for the first time, he thought that being with Harper was an on-going learning experience.

Chapter Fourteen

As it turned out, the rain that was projected never materialized. Consequently, what was supposed to be only a short picnic wound up being an all-day, exhausting affair. Because of that, the twins ran themselves totally ragged. They certainly outlasted a number of other children whose parents and families had also thought that a short spring picnic was a really good idea.

"You have a really lovely family, my dear," one sweet-faced grandmother warmly commented to Harper as she and Brady were carrying the exhausted twins to the car.

Harper opened her mouth to protest that neither the twins nor Brady were hers, but then she decided that the situation was too complicated to explain quickly. Besides, the older woman appeared to be taking such satisfaction in the picture they made. The woman was literally beaming at them.

So, in response to that, Harper merely told the woman "Thank you," and proceeded with the sleeping Tyler to the car.

"You know," Harper said quietly as she carefully eased Tyler into his car seat and then securely fastened his seat belt around his small body, "I don't think I've *ever* seen either one of the twins so quiet. I think that running around in the open like this really drained them—a lot."

"I think we might have stumbled onto something," Brady joked. Toby murmured something against his shoulder as Brady put the twin into his car seat. He stood back and regarded the sleeping boys. "They look like angels, don't they?" he asked Harper. "Nobody would ever guess what little devils these guys can actually be." He smoothed Toby's hair back from his forehead. His smile faded as he paused and looked at the twin thoughtfully. "Hey, Harper?"

"Yes?" she asked, preoccupied as she checked the seat belts a second time to be absolutely sure they were secure.

Brady was still looking dubiously at Toby. "Is Toby supposed to be this warm?"

The concern in Brady's voice caught her attention. She did what she could to reassure him. "Well, he has been running around all day so he's bound to be warm," she told Brady as she leaned over the boy to make sure everything was all right.

She fell back on the timeless, tried-and-true method to determine whether or not a child was running a fever. She kissed his forehead. However, the moment she did, Harper shook her head.

"But Toby shouldn't be *this* warm," she told Brady.

"So you think he has a fever?" Brady asked her, his stomach making itself into a knot as he anticipated her answer.

"I *know* he has a fever," Harper answered. There was no room for an argument in her tone. "Let's get these two guys home," she told Brady as she handed him her keys. "Here, you drive." Accepting the car keys, he looked at Harper quizzically. She knew what he was about to ask. "I want to be able to turn around in my seat and keep my eye on the twins in case they need something."

Twins. Plural. Alarms immediately went off in Brady's head.

"Does Tyler have a fever, too?" he asked apprehensively.

"Not that I can tell, but they did run around

together all day." She saw the apprehensive look wash over Brady's face. She did what she could to reassure him. "That doesn't necessarily mean that they're both going to get sick," she said as he started up the car.

Brady knew that he needed something to cling to, no matter how thin. "It doesn't?"

She realized what he was asking her—and why. Harper rose to the occasion. "No, I've known one kid to come down with the flu while his sibling, sleeping only a few feet away, didn't even get so much as a cough or a sore throat, much less come down with anything more serious."

Brady appreciated her effort. It hit him that he came from a large family. He had grown up surrounded by siblings. "How did I miss all this growing up?" he upbraided himself.

"Don't beat yourself up," Harper told him. "Kids are usually self-centered and don't really pay attention to anything around them. It's normal," she assured Brady. "And another thing you might not be aware of, a lot of kids run a temperature in the morning, then it's gone in the afternoon, only to reappear in the evening. It's all part of a pattern. For the most part, kids are really resilient." Harper's eyes met his as he came to a red light and turned around to look at her. "It's going to be okay," she promised Brady.

Toby suddenly stirred, moaned and then opened his eyes. Harper looked at the boy more closely. She could see that his eyes were watery.

"Harper," Toby said in a raspy voice that made it sound as if he was on the verge of crying. "I don't feel so good."

"We're taking you home, honey. You're going to be okay," she told the twin firmly. Harper twisted around in her seat so that she could hold the boy's hand.

It felt hot, just like the rest of him.

"Drive a little faster, Brady," she told him in a calm voice that belied the concern she was feeling.

"I'll take him up to his room," Harper volunteered when Brady pulled up in his driveway. "You bring up Tyler."

"Maybe they should be in separate rooms," Brady suggested. He felt totally at a loss as to how to handle any of this.

"I think that's kind of like closing the barn door after the horse got out," she replied. "They're always together so Tyler has been exposed already. If he's going to get sick, he will," she told Brady as she carried Toby to the front door.

Holding Tyler against his shoulder with one

hand, Brady quickly unlocked the front door for her with the other.

"I already checked out Tyler," she told Brady, "and he doesn't feel warm to me."

Walking into the house, she carried Toby up the stairs and into his room. She set him on the bed, then very carefully took off his clothes and put him into his pajamas. The boy slept through most of it, waking up for a moment only to fall back asleep.

Brady stood back, looking really concerned. "Maybe we should take him to the hospital," he said as he changed Tyler into his pajamas.

"It's probably just a cold or maybe the flu," she told Brady. "I'll go get the thermometer so we can see what we're up against."

Because Toby had fallen asleep, Harper took the boy's temperature under his armpit. She adjusted her reading because of the thermometer's location.

Despite how hot his head felt, Toby's temperature wasn't registering all that high.

But Brady still didn't feel better about the situation. "I can't stand to see him like this," he told Harper as he looked down at Toby. The twin looked incredibly small and vulnerable to him. "Look, I know you usually go home at the end of the day, but would you mind staying, you know, the night?"

Damn, he sounded like some awkward teen-ager, Brady thought, annoyed with himself. He decided to level with her and confessed, "I'm really out of my element here. I'll pay you over-time," he quickly offered.

"You don't have to pay me overtime," she told him, waving the suggestion away. This was not about the money. It never had been. "I'll be happy to stay with Toby."

"You will?" Brady looked visibly relieved. He needed someone here who knew what they were doing. "You have no idea how grateful I am."

Harper smiled at him. "Oh, I think I can guess. Why don't you go to bed and get some sleep?" she suggested, then told him, "I'll stay in here with the boys."

Brady looked around the room as if he hadn't seen it before. "But there's no bed for you," he pointed out.

"No, but there is a recliner," she said. It had been the first thing to catch her eye when she had initially seen the room. "Don't worry. I'll make do," Harper assured him. "Now go to bed. He'll probably wake up tomorrow morning with energy to spare."

He looked at the boy's tiny face, concern evi-dent on his own. "I hope you're right," he told her.

"I'll remind you that you said that," she prom-ised with a smile. "Now go, get some rest."

"Okay."

Exhausted and drained, Brady left the room, convinced he wasn't going to get a wink of sleep.

He was asleep a second after his head hit the pillow.

Brady woke up with a start.

It was morning.

How did that happen? he upbraided himself. Somehow, he had slept straight through the night. That hardly ever happened anymore. At least, not in the last six months.

Awake now, thoughts of Toby flooded his brain. Guilt was less than half a beat behind.

Looking down at himself, Brady realized that he had fallen asleep in his clothes. Since he had, there was no need to get dressed. He even had on his shoes.

Brady quickly made his way to the twins' room.

He found Harper there and she was already awake, looking uncommonly fresh, especially given the situation.

That only succeeded in making him feel twice as guilty as he already did.

Moving as quietly as possible, Brady came up behind Harper and asked her, "How is he?"

"Well, he still has a fever," she told him, not wanting to hide anything from Brady. "But the good news is Tyler seems fine. When Toby wakes up, I'm going to give him a sponge bath, try to lower his temperature."

"The hospital—"

"Will still be there if we decide to take him as another option later. But at the moment, I don't think there's a reason to panic. I'll make him drink a lot of liquids. I'll watch him and if his fever goes up or he gets worse, we can take him in then. But in my experience, that's a last resort."

He didn't know if he was up to this waiting game. "Why don't we just take him in now?" Brady wanted to know.

"Because we might not have to," Harper explained. "And I don't think you want to teach him to panic at the first sign that he might be coming down with something," she added.

"But—"

"You want to raise these boys to learn how to take things in stride," Harper advised, then asked, "Don't you?"

She was making sense, Brady thought, nodding his head. "You're right," he agreed, then looked down at Toby. "I guess this whole thing just made me lose my head."

She laughed softly and gave his hand a quick, warm squeeze. "Face it. You're a first-time parent and you got into the game late. Reacting the way you did is just a sign that you care," Harper told him. "And in case that fact managed to escape you, that's a good thing."

He blew out a long breath. Becoming the twins' guardian had made for a rough six months, but to date this was by far the roughest thing he had gone through. "I'd go to pieces if you weren't here, you know that, don't you?" he asked Harper.

To his surprise, she shook her head. "No, you'd get on the phone to one of your married cousins or siblings and you'd ask for their advice," she contradicted. "And then you'd get through this."

He wasn't buying it. She was an important part in his being able to handle this. "Don't sell yourself short. If you weren't here, I'd be a complete basket case by now," he told Harper.

"No, you wouldn't be," she insisted. "But instead of arguing with me, why don't you go down and make us some breakfast?" Harper suggested.

He laughed at the idea. She had to know better, he thought. In case she didn't, he asked her, "I take it you have your heart set on coming down with a case of ptomaine poisoning."

Harper smiled, taking him at his word. "That bad, huh?"

"Well, I can open a cereal box," Brady responded. "And the refrigerator to take out a carton of milk, but not much else."

She shook her head, totally amazed at his inability to do something she considered to be so simple. Scrambling eggs. But then, she had been the one to do the shopping, she recalled. Prior to her first trip to the grocery store, there hadn't been all that much in the refrigerator, she reminded herself.

"You stay with the boys. I'll go and grab a quick shower," she told him, beginning to leave the room.

"Um, Harper?"

She turned around and looked at Brady. He looked utterly lost again, she thought. "What do I do if he wakes up?"

She didn't understand his problem. "Same thing you've been doing when he wakes up."

"But he's sick now," Brady protested.

She still didn't understand. "Hasn't he ever been sick before?" Harper asked incredulously.

"Not really. He had a slight cold once, but that didn't slow him down. But now..." His voice trailed off as he looked at the boy. Suddenly, Toby looked almost terribly lost in his bed.

Brady couldn't remember ever feeling so helpless in his entire life.

"If he wakes up, you take hold of his hand and tell him that everything's going to be all right."

She looked at him with sympathy. She imagined this had to be hard on Brady. "Really sell it," she advised, then asked, "Anything else?"

"No," Brady answered. He was up to this, he told himself. Everything was going to be all right.

"Be back soon," Harper promised.

She wasn't gone five minutes when Toby moaned and opened his eyes. Brady's first instinct was to call for Harper.

Instead, he made his way over to Toby. "How are you feeling, soldier?" he asked the lethargic-looking little boy.

Huge puppy-dog eyes looked up at him. "Terrible," he complained.

"Well, you'll be back to your old self before you know it," Brady promised, trying to sound as positive as possible.

Tyler was up and he crawled up next to him as he asked, worried, "He's not going to die, is he?"

"No, he's not going to die, Tyler," he told the boy. "Whatever made you ask something like that?"

"You looked so worried," Tyler answered. "I thought that maybe…maybe…" He sniffled. "Well, you know."

Yes, he knew, Brady thought. The boy had let his imagination get the better of him. "Don't worry, Ty." He hugged the boy to him. "Toby will be back to his old self very soon."

Tyler rolled that over in his head. "Can it not be too soon?" he asked.

"Why would you say that?" he wanted to know.

Tyler tugged on the bottom of Brady's sweatshirt, beckoning him to bend down to his level. "He's nicer this way. Doesn't call me any funny names or anything," he whispered.

"Well, when your brother gets better, we'll have a talk with him about that," Brady promised. That seemed to placate Tyler. "All right, boys, what would you like for breakfast?" he asked, doing his best to pretend everything was going as usual.

Toby, who looked as if he was slipping in and out of consciousness, stared up at Brady. He shook his head. "I'm not hungry."

"Now there's a first," he said, trying to lighten the mood because Tyler looked apprehensive as he stared at his brother. Toby had always been an eating machine.

"Maybe we should take him to the hospital," Brady murmured, feeling uneasy about the situation. What if he got really bad?

"Hospital?" Tyler cried, his voice going up. The word hospital made him think of his parents. His grandmother had told him that his parents had been taken to the hospital and had died there. The facts had gotten muddled, but the effect remained. "Is he going to die?" the little boy cried, his eyes welling up immediately.

"No, he's not going to die," Brady said firmly, trying to reassure Tyler. "I'm just a little worried, but we're not going to the hospital yet. Let's wait a little and see if your brother can get better on his own," he told Tyler.

He fervently hoped he wasn't being too lax. By the same token, he didn't want Tyler to panic.

Brady looked toward the door, willing Harper to come back and take over. She had a way of making everything seem as if it was going to be all right.

He never needed to be reassured more than he did right at this moment.

Chapter Fifteen

All things considered, Toby's fever cleared up rather quickly. But it was obvious to Harper that the little boy wasn't back to his normal self. Whatever he had come down with was lingering in his system. The mischievous glint was gone from his eyes and his behavior was entirely subdued.

That was when she put in a call to the recently built Rambling Rose Pediatric Center and asked to speak to the boys' pediatrician, Wayne Patterson. She wanted to be sure she wasn't being too laid-back about the whole thing. The doctor himself came on the phone. He listened quietly to her narrative, then said something that put her mind at ease, indicating that he was on top of the situation.

"Sounds like Toby caught what's been making the rounds lately," Dr. Patterson told her. "You say that Toby's fever only lasted for the day and that it's gone now?"

"Yes, but he doesn't have any of his usual energy," she told the doctor.

"That's normal, too," the doctor confirmed. "Just keep him resting for as long as possible. Be sure to give him plenty of liquids and see that he eats well. No junk food," Dr. Patterson specified. "This should run its course in a few days, tops. If it doesn't, or he starts to regress, call my office immediately and bring him in. But between the two of us, I don't think you have anything to worry about," the doctor concluded.

That was a relief, Harper thought. She had begun to think that she was being too blasé. "Thank you, Doctor."

"My pleasure, Ms. Radcliffe," the pediatrician replied.

Though heartened by the pediatrician's prognosis, Harper still remained at the house for the duration of Toby's confinement. Tyler, too, stayed with his brother, no doubt still concerned. For the most part, rather than video games, she had all of them playing simple board games that the twins had brought with them when they moved to Rambling Rose.

When they grew tired of playing those, she read stories to them, holding Toby and Tyler captive by doing different voices for the various characters in the stories.

Since she was there, keeping the twins occupied, this allowed Brady to continue working at the hotel. But he made a point of trying to keep his hours reasonable so he could get home before either of the twins was asleep. He felt it only fair to provide Harper with at least temporary relief since she had agreed to stay at his house.

However, today Brady was unable to come home as early as he had the two previous days, although he did call to check on Toby's condition. When he finally did get home, no one was downstairs in the family room or the living room.

Growing apprehensive—had Toby gotten worse and been taken to the emergency room?—he went looking for her and the twins.

Taking the stairs, he experienced a sense of relief when he heard what sounded like a rollicking story being played out.

And then he heard the twins laughing.

Both of them, he realized.

That meant that Toby had to be getting better,

he thought, pleased. He hadn't heard Toby laugh since the boy had gotten sick.

Brady took the rest of the stairs two at a time. From the sound of it, he expected to find Harper and the boys gathered around the small TV he had brought into the twins' room.

When he reached the bedroom doorway, Brady was surprised to discover that there was no television program or Blu-ray Disc being played. All the different voices he had heard were coming from one source.

Harper.

Fascinated, he stood just shy of the doorway, listening to the story she told for several minutes—until Tyler looked up and became aware of his presence.

"Unca Brady, you're home!" the boy cried, running up and then throwing his arms around Brady's waist, hugging him as hard as he could.

Surprised as well as pleased, Brady smiled down at the boy, giving Tyler a hug back.

"It sure looks that way," Brady said to the boy. One arm around Tyler's shoulders, he guided the boy back to Toby's bed. "So how are you two feeling?" he asked the twins.

"Great!" Tyler cried with enthusiasm. He had never caught Toby's flu.

"I'm getting better all the time," Toby proudly

announced, then pouted, "But Harper won't let me get out of bed to play."

"Harper's a wise lady," Brady told the boy solemnly. "If I were you, I'd listen to what she has to say."

It was obvious that Toby clearly thought he was missing out on something. But instead of arguing with Brady—or Harper—he just sighed dramatically, a clear sign to Brady that the boy still wasn't operating at a hundred percent of his normal energy.

Well, he'd take what he could get, Brady thought. He glanced toward Harper, thinking that the woman had to have supernatural powers. There was no other explanation for Toby's behavior.

Harper took advantage of the slight lull. "Have you eaten yet?" she asked Brady.

He shook his head. "I came straight home so I could see these guys before you put them to bed," he confessed, smiling at the twins again. "Work ran long today," he said, explaining why he had arrived home later than he had the last few days.

Harper nodded. "Well, I left dinner on the stove, waiting for you. I'll go down and heat it up a little while you visit with the boys. Then, when I come upstairs, we'll trade places and you can go down and have dinner. How's that sound?" she wanted to know.

"Yes, ma'am, that sounds fine," Brady responded, saluting her.

The twins dissolved in a fit of giggles, as if they had been privy to a great joke.

Their response warmed Brady's heart. He realized how much he had missed the sound of their combined laughter these last few days.

He also realized, when he went back downstairs a little later after Harper had warmed up dinner, just how right all of this felt to him: coming home at night to find Harper there. Waking up in the morning to the sound of her moving around, usually in the kitchen, preparing breakfast for everyone.

It wasn't the meals—which were always uncommonly good—it was her presence in the house that made the difference. That made his house feel like a real home. He knew he really didn't want to go back to the way things were.

"Well, I think I finally got them to both fall asleep," Harper announced when she walked into the kitchen some thirty minutes later.

Brady had just finished eating the dinner she had warmed up for him. "Great. Sorry, I didn't mean to disrupt your nighttime routine," he apologized.

"You didn't disrupt it," she told him with a warm smile. "You coming in at that time was only a slight setback. Besides, this is your house," Harper reminded him. "You have a right to come in any time you want, you know."

He really wanted her to know what a difference she had made in all their lives. "You know that I appreciate you doing all this. I couldn't have managed any of this without you. I couldn't have *survived* all this without you," he amended with emphasis.

Her eyes crinkled as her smile grew wider. "Glad I could help."

"Yes, about that…" Brady began, searching for the right words to take advantage of the opening she had just given him.

Harper was about to pick up his empty plates. Something in his voice stopped her and she looked at Brady. "Yes?"

Here goes nothing, he thought. "Will you reconsider becoming a live-in nanny?"

She didn't answer immediately. Instead, Harper thought of all the complications that had arisen at her last job. Being a live-in nanny for the Wheelers had ended with unwanted advances, a terrible misunderstanding and an ultimate boot from her job.

Harper took a breath. "My immediate answer," she told him honestly, "would be no."

Brady realized that it would mean extra work and he thought that was what she was talking about. "I wouldn't expect you to say yes without offering you compensation for the extra time," he told her.

She shook her head. He didn't understand, she thought. "It's not about the money," Harper told him.

He stopped her right there. "I understand that. It's about the twins. But you have to know that they function so much better when you're around. You can make them do things that I just can't. In the few short weeks that you've been part of their lives, you've gotten Toby and Tyler to listen, to sit still and to, if not behave, then to *almost* behave." He laughed dryly. "I don't have to worry if the house will still be standing when I get home at night."

"Now you're exaggerating," she told him.

Brady's dark eyes met hers. "Am I?" he wanted to know.

"Well, at least a little," she allowed with that easy laugh of hers that always seemed to get to him.

He decided to lean on her good will. "It would really be helping me out," Brady told her. "And not only that, but it would also be great for the twins. C'mon," he coaxed. "What do you say? At least give it a trial run. You've got nothing to lose," Brady reasoned, "and the twins would be thrilled to have you around all the time."

She had never been good at saying no and she was having more and more trouble saying no to Brady. That in itself worried her, but for now she pushed that aside and into the background.

"Well," Harper said slowly, already beginning to relent, "I guess I can give it a try."

"Terrific! I promise you won't regret it," he told her enthusiastically.

Brady almost forgot himself and reached out to hug Harper, but he knew that would be totally unprofessional. Stepping over the line.

So he held himself in check. The last thing he wanted was to give her the wrong idea about him—even though it could, just possibly, be the right one. The truth of it was, he did find himself having feelings for her. But those feelings could very well destroy the best thing he had accidentally stumbled across.

A loving nanny for the twins.

So he restrained himself and merely offered Harper his hand.

"Here's to a really great working arrangement," Brady told her, the corners of his mouth curving.

"At least temporarily so," she qualified, shaking the hand he offered.

Brady laughed, finally rising from the table. He was holding his empty dinner dishes. "I'll tell you one thing. You do keep a man on his toes," he said.

She raised an eyebrow. "You mean off-balance?" she asked as she took the dishes from him. Harper brought them over to the sink.

"Yeah, that, too," he agreed, laughing.

Because it was true, he thought. She did keep him off-balance. But lately, especially after these four trying days, he was beginning to find himself leaning in a certain direction, a direction that no longer placed such emphasis on being a bachelor, carefree or otherwise. More important things were beginning to take front and center in his life. Namely the twins—and Harper.

Within another day, Toby's illness was a thing of the past. Very quickly, he was back at preschool and back to his former, very energized self.

"Guess what!" Toby cried, bouncing up and down one afternoon when Harper came to pick him and his twin up from preschool.

Two days had gone by since he had returned to school and it was as if he couldn't even remember ever being sick.

Harper pretended to concentrate in order to come up with an answer. "Your teacher was finally able to tell you and your brother apart?" she teased.

"No, she still can't do that," Toby told her. "But that's not exciting," he pointed out.

Yes, he was definitely back to his old self, Harper thought. She noticed that Tyler looked as if he was bursting with news, as well. Any second now, she knew the twins were going to start competing with one another and jockeying for position.

"All right, spill it. What's so exciting?" Harper asked the boys.

Toby and Tyler answered her in unison. "We're gonna be in the school pa-pa—in the school play," they finally said.

She'd heard that there was going to be a spring pageant, but she thought that was just something that they meant for parents and children to attend and she planned to join the boys and Brady. The thought of actually seeing Toby and Tyler on the stage, performing, had never occurred to her.

"Really?" she asked, mentally taking her hat off to the brave teacher who was going to be in charge of herding the little darlings onto the stage.

"Yeah, really. Guess what we're going to be," Toby said, dancing from foot to foot.

She shook her head. "I don't have a single idea. What?" she asked.

"I'll give you a hint," Toby told her magnanimously. And then he hopped.

"Rabbits?" Harper guessed.

"No!" they cried together. This time they both hopped, then Toby loudly cried, "Rib-bit!"

"We're green," Tyler hinted, lowering his voice.

"Frogs?" Harper guessed, playing along.

"Yeah!" Toby happily declared. "We're frogs. You gotta make our costumes," the twin added as if she should have already known that.

Terrific, Harper thought. She forced a smile to her lips, then said, "Great."

Tyler, ever the practical one, suddenly looked at her and asked, concerned, "You know how to make costumes, right?"

There was no doubt about it. The boy just warmed her heart, Harper thought. "Lucky for you, yes, I do." At least well enough to *pass* for a costume, she thought.

"Teacher says we've gotta learn our lies. Can you help us with that, too?" Toby wanted to know.

Lies? And then it hit her. "Lines, Toby. The word is *lines*. And yes I can," she told him.

He nodded, then looked a little mystified and asked, "What's lines, Harper?"

"Lines are the words you're supposed to say when you're on the stage."

"Learning lines sounds hard," Tyler decided.

She didn't want them getting disillusioned so

easily. "Not really," she told the twins. "It's like a game. It'll be fun," she promised them.

Tyler beamed at her. "Everything's fun with you, Harper."

"Thank you," Harper replied, giving the boys one huge hug. "I feel the same way about you."

"Do you think Unca Brady will want to come to see us be frogs?" Tyler asked.

"Oh, I know he will," Harper answered.

"But he's gonna be working," Tyler worried. "We gotta do it in the daytime."

"Oh, he'll find time for this," Harper promised the little boys. "He wouldn't dream of missing you guys."

"You really think so?" Toby asked, dubious.

"I know so," she assured the boys. She saw Toby and Tyler exchanging looks and grins.

When they grinned like that, it was usually a sign that they were up to something. But for the life of her, Harper hadn't a clue what that could be. For now, she put that sort of thing on the back burner.

"C'mon, boys. Let's go see your teacher so I can get a copy of the script and help you two memorize your lines."

"Yeah, let's!" Toby declared as he and Tyler both took one of her hands in theirs and went back to their classroom.

Chapter Sixteen

"Did ya see us? Did ya see?" Toby cried, all but flying off the stage after the class performance was over. The people in the audience were still applauding, but both the twins were excited and eager to find out how the two most important adults in their lives liked seeing them in the play.

"Yes, we certainly did see you," Brady answered, glancing at Harper. The latter was beaming her approval at the twins. "You were both fantastic!" he said.

"You were the most adorable, believable frogs I have ever seen," Harper said, adding her voice to Brady's. Turning her head so that only Brady could hear her, she whispered, "And their teacher did a brilliant job harnessing all that little-boy energy of theirs and putting it to good use."

"You can sure say that again," Brady agreed with a laugh.

"Say what again? Huh? Say what?" Toby asked, his head popping up in Brady's direction, all but whirling around, first going toward Brady, then to his nanny, finally back again.

"That you were both brilliant playing those frogs," Harper said, thinking fast.

Spotting their uncle Adam and his wife, Laurel, the twins waved at the pair. "There's Larkin's mommy and daddy," Tyler told Harper, pointing them out to her in case she didn't see the couple.

"Honey," Harper began, pretending to grow serious with the boy, "what did I say about pointing to people?"

For the space of a second, Tyler hung his head. "Not to," he answered solemnly. Still, to him pointing out their family seemed like something perfectly normal for him to do.

What Tyler said next caught both her and Brady totally by surprise.

"When you and Unca Brady get married, can we be a family like them?" Tyler wanted to know.

Harper felt all the air completely rush out of her lungs, leaving her somewhat dizzy and disoriented.

Brady saw the expression on Harper's face. She looked as if she had just seen a ghost. He hadn't a clue why she was reacting that way. Did she find the idea of being with him so terribly distasteful, he wondered.

He was going to have to ask her about that later. Right now he felt that he had to say something to keep the twins from asking Harper a lot of possibly uncomfortable questions.

Maybe it was his imagination, but he couldn't help thinking that she seemed as if she wanted to bolt.

"Hold it, boys. Nobody's getting married. Harper is your nanny, not my girlfriend," he reminded the twins pointedly.

Tyler looked at Harper, obviously disappointed. "Is that true?"

Harper nodded. *Nice save*, she thought, although at the same time, she felt a twinge of disappointment herself. "I'm afraid so," she answered out loud.

She needed this job and she knew that the kids needed her. And Brady, she thought, needed her to keep the kids reined in.

Even so, right now all she wanted to do was run away as fast as she could.

Harper closed her eyes for a second, doing her best to exercise control over her reaction. Otherwise, she was going to make herself crazy.

Because she didn't know what else to do, Harper found herself beginning to put up walls between herself and Brady.

But even doing that somehow didn't feel right to her.

For the next few days she did what she could to focus on the job as well as on the twins—and on nothing beyond that. Especially not on their handsome guardian.

But it wasn't easy, especially when circumstances kept throwing her and Brady together.

Circumstances like the upcoming Easter holiday and all that entailed.

As was to be expected, the twins had outgrown their nicer clothes, which meant that Harper needed to take them shopping for new outfits.

"Do we gotta go shopping?" Toby complained, fidgeting at the very thought of having to get new clothes.

"Tell me, do you want to get Easter baskets?" she asked the twins.

"Yeah!" the boys cried in unison.

"Well," Harper told the duo seriously, "the Easter Bunny told me that only good little girls and boys who wear their brand-new Easter outfits will be getting those Easter baskets."

The twins looked at each other, stunned. "For real?" they questioned.

She nodded her head solemnly. "For real," she told them.

Toby sighed as he looked at his brother. And then speaking for both of them, he said in a totally resigned voice, "Well, I guess if we gotta, we gotta."

Glancing over her shoulder, Harper flashed a smile at Brady. The latter looked very impressed. In his experience, even the twins' parents couldn't manage them the way that Harper could.

Since it was a Saturday, all four of them drove to the local shopping center to go shopping.

Once in the store, Harper swiftly made a number of selections for the twins to try on.

Tyler surprised them by keeping a positive outlook on this unwanted excursion. "And if we get new Easter clothes, does that mean we can go on the Easter egg hunt at Unca Brady's hotel?"

"It's not my hotel," Brady corrected the boy. "But yes, if you two get new Easter outfits, you can go on the Easter egg hunt." It seemed like the perfect trade-off, he thought.

Getting the go-ahead on that succeeded in firing up the twins' imagination. "Can we get a pet rabbit, too?" Tyler wanted to know.

Not waiting for his brother to get an answer,

Toby jumped in with a question of his own and, in typical twin fashion, he upped the stakes. "How about a pony? Can we get a pet pony?" he asked eagerly.

Not to be outdone, Tyler piped up with another request of his own. "I want a pet dinosaur."

Meanwhile, as these negotiations were going on, Harper was subtly getting the twins to try on the outfits she had chosen. She eased each boy into the clothes as she continued to distract them by getting them to talk about the pets they wanted Brady to get them.

"What kind of dinosaur?" she asked innocently, as if buying one was actually even a possibility.

"A big one!" Tyler cried.

"Yeah, a big one," Toby yelled enthusiastically. "And green! We want a green one!" he declared.

Damn but she was good, Brady thought, admiring the way Harper worked. She was stimulating their imaginations so that they didn't even realize that she was getting them to try on the various outfits.

The woman really had skills. Brady silently tipped his hat to her.

A passing saleswoman paused to watch this mini-performance with costume changes and nodded with approval. "Your wife is really very good with your children," she told him. "Most parents I see around here, especially around the holidays, usually wind up losing their tempers, screaming at their kids to behave and stop squirming around while they're getting them to try on new outfits."

The saleswoman smiled as she nodded at Harper. "You've really got yourself a good one here," she told him. Then she turned to the twins. "You boys listen to your mama." The woman eyed the outfits that Harper had draped on the side of a chair. "Looks like she's found some really nice clothes for you to wear for Easter." Digging into her pocket, the older woman took out two little plastic bags. Each was filled with a rainbow of jellybeans. "Is it all right if I give them these little bags of jellybeans?"

Harper saw the eager, pleading look on the twins' faces. "Yes."

The twins practically cheered as the woman said, "Here you go, boys," and handed each twin a bag. "Happy Easter."

The title the saleswoman had bestowed on her had Harper flustered. "I'm not their mother," she told the woman. "I'm their nanny."

The woman took the correction in stride. "Oh. My apologies," she said. "I meant no disrespect." She looked at Harper and Brady. Her expression seemed to say that if they weren't a couple, they should be. "It's just that you all made such a perfect picture."

"Pictures are just illusions," Harper told the woman a little too quickly.

"Of course." The saleswoman offered her an embarrassed smile and retreated.

Picking up the clothes that Harper had ultimately selected for the twins, Brady followed behind her and the twins, going to the register.

Harper's reaction to the saleswoman's assumption bothered him. "Just what is your problem?" he asked Harper under his breath, placing his credit card down beside the pile of clothing.

Afraid that this might wind up quickly escalating into something extremely awkward, Harper placed herself between Brady and the boys.

She seemed to almost be shielding them with her body, he thought.

"This is not the time or the place to talk about this," she informed Brady between gritted teeth.

"Fair enough," he agreed as he signed his name on the bottom of the sales receipt. "But this isn't over," Brady informed her. "We're going to talk about this again—and very soon."

A chill ran down her spine. Harper didn't answer him. Instead, placing a hand on each of their shoulders, she ushered the boys out of the store. That left Brady to follow behind, carrying the bags.

He brought the bags over to the car and put them into his trunk.

Because he didn't want to upset the twins—and he did want to be able to talk to Harper freely—Brady waited until he drove them all home.

The twins didn't even take any notice of the silence. They were too busy filling the car with their exuberant, high voices.

But Brady noticed the silence.

As did Harper.

The moment he pulled up in the driveway and the twins were freed from their car seat restraints, the duo bolted into the backyard.

Brady took out the shopping bags and carried them into the house, then left them in the living room. Once he was confident that the twins were playing and occupied, and he and Harper were alone, he cornered Harper, picking up their unfinished conversation.

"Okay, just what was all that about in the store?" Brady wanted to know. When she didn't answer him immediately, he pressed, "Why were you acting so weird?"

"I wasn't acting weird," Harper denied, her voice going up.

Avoiding his eyes, she moved about the kitchen, preparing everyone's lunch.

But Brady wasn't about to back down. As she went from counter to stove, then to the refrigerator, he continued to follow her around. He was determined to get a straight answer out of her.

When she still didn't say anything, he informed her, "Then you weren't in the same conversation as I was back in that store."

He was just going to keep following her until she gave him some sort of an answer, Harper thought, so she turned to him. "All right, maybe I was being a little erratic back there," she admitted. "But you have to understand, I just can't risk another fiasco."

"*Another* fiasco?" Brady echoed. "What was the first one?"

She really hadn't wanted to get into this. With no choice, she gave him an abbreviated version of what had transpired with her last position.

"The last family I worked for, the situation got a little…dicey," she concluded. "It finally got to the point where I decided that I had to leave—"

"What happened?" he wanted to know.

She wasn't ready to get into that. "It doesn't matter," she told him. "What matters is that leaving was very difficult. The little girls I was taking care of…they cried when I left." As she said it, she felt like she was reliving the whole ordeal.

It became almost difficult for her to breathe. "They had gotten too attached to me," she confided.

What she didn't add was that she was afraid that she was getting too attached to Brady and the twins—and that carried its own set of consequences with it.

"I see," Brady responded, thinking the situation over. "Okay," he decided, "maybe I let all this get out of hand." Although he really didn't believe that, it was obvious that Harper did. So, for now, until he could resolve this satisfactorily, Brady humored her. "I'll just remind the kids that it's your job to be with them and nothing more."

He saw that what he had just said had made her wince. Can't win for losing, he thought.

"Now what?" he asked out loud.

"Well, I'm afraid when you put it that way, it makes me sound so…mercenary," she finally complained.

At his wit's end, Brady threw up his hands in frustration. "Women can really be so damn confusing!" he cried.

"I'm not confusing," Harper all but snapped. "Don't you understand? I just don't want Tyler and Toby to get hurt." *Or me, either*, she added silently.

"Well, they wouldn't be if you didn't keep going up and then down and then up again about all of this. It's like trying to keep my eye on a yo-yo or a…"

His voice trailed off as he suddenly looked at her from a brand-new perspective. "Hey, I know what's going on here," he declared as things began coming together in his head.

"What?" she asked apprehensively, not knowing what to expect.

Brady grinned. "You like me." He said it as if it was the final answer to a puzzle.

"Well, of course I like you," she told him. And then it suddenly occurred to her what he meant by that. Harper quickly took back what she'd just said. "But I don't *like* you. Not like that," she cried.

She was scared. He could understand that. In a way, he had to admit that he was, too.

Brady pulled away, letting his hand fall to hers. "I'm sorry. I didn't mean to overstep."

Harper responded, "I know you didn't. Neither of us did. This is mutual. Brady—I just don't want to get carried away."

He met her gaze, and he could see that she was feeling the same conflicted emotions he was. Longing. Desire. Hesitation. It was in her eyes, and the way she had worded her protest.

"Neither do I." His voice was soft, coaxing. Skimming along her skin seductively. And then, just like that, almost against his will, he finally did what he had been dying to do for days now.

He kissed Harper.

As she felt his kiss's effects all but explode throughout her entire body, Harper tried to get a grip on both herself and the situation.

Pulling away from him, she put her hand on Brady's chest, keeping him at bay. "Brady, maybe we shouldn't be doing this," she told him breathlessly. But she knew her words were a lame attempt to put a wall up against the swell of need she felt—and wanted to give in to. Her fingers remained on Brady's chest, feeling him breathe.

Despite what she said, he could see that she wanted this as much as he did. It was in her eyes, and in the way she had worded her protest. But he didn't try to talk her out of pulling away. He just continued looking at her.

And just like that, they were back in each other's arms, kissing again.

Somehow, they had managed to get onto the sofa and the situation only grew hotter and more demanding from that point on.

Passion grew as he went on kissing her. The moment, the feeling, just continued to escalate until they found themselves tottering on the apex of the moment.

Breathing heavily, Brady drew back for a second, knowing that any second now, they would be crossing a line that he hadn't really considered crossing—until just now.

A line that, once crossed, would result in changing everything.

But as he leaned back in, ready to continue, ready to change the entire dynamic of their relationship, it was Harper who surprised him. She put her hands on his shoulders and pushed him back.

Confused, bewildered, Brady looked at her, an obvious question in his eyes.

"I can't," she told him again. "I just can't let this happen." She was crying now and seeing her like that, suffering like that, almost succeeded in breaking Brady's heart.

He tried his best to comfort her, but she shook her head, getting up from the sofa.

"I have to leave," she told him, her voice almost breaking.

Brady didn't understand what she was telling him. "The room?"

Harper shook her head. "No. Here. You, the kids. I have to leave," she repeated, tears sliding down her cheeks.

"But what *about* the kids?" he asked her, trying to make sense of what she was telling him. She kept pointing out how happy being a nanny made her. What was going on here? "They'll be devastated. Not to mention that they'll feel abandoned. And I have to work," he reminded her. "I need you to be here with the twins."

"I won't leave you in the lurch," she told him. "I'll look after them until you can find someone else to take care of them. But I can't live here anymore," she told him. "I'm going to move out," she said in case that wasn't clear.

And then she quickly left the room before she lost her nerve.

Chapter Seventeen

Harper went through the motions of preparing a full dinner for the family as if nothing had happened. For the most part, Brady stayed out of her way, but he did peek into the kitchen a couple of times to make sure that everything was going well—and that she hadn't abruptly left.

When he saw that she was still there, still cooking, he began to hope that maybe Harper had changed her mind about leaving after all. Maybe life might actually go back to what it had been before all this had gone down.

Brady mentally crossed his fingers. After all, if she actually left, he didn't know what he would do without her. He realized that he had grown to care for her a great deal.

However, at the dinner table, Brady noticed that the twins did almost all of the talking, going from one thing to another like bees that couldn't make up their minds which flower to land on.

For her part, Harper hardly said anything at all and that really worried him. He was at a loss as to how to make the situation right without making her feel that he was crowding her.

After dinner was over and Harper had cleared away all the dishes and washed them, instead of joining them in the living room where Brady was playing a game with Toby and Tyler the way she usually did, or taking them out for an evening walk, Harper quietly withdrew and disappeared into her room.

The twins were having an argument over the plot of a cartoon they had watched earlier, but seeing Harper leave the room had brought their "discussion" to a skidding halt.

Tyler looked at Brady, concern etched into his small face. "Is Harper sick?" he wanted to know.

"What makes you think that?" Brady asked, wanting to avoid discussing what was going on with the boys if he possibly could. He sought for a way to redirect the conversation.

"She *always* plays with us," Toby stressed,

speaking up. And then he pointed out the obvious. "She's not playing with us now."

Sensing that the boys needed to talk about it, Brady came as close to the truth as he could. "I think she just wants some time to herself." Mentally, he crossed his fingers that that was all there was to it.

"Did going shopping with us make her tired?" Tyler wanted to know, concern puckering his small face.

"Something like that," Brady answered vaguely.

"Well, I'm going to go and cheer her up," Toby announced. And before Brady could stop him, the twin took off.

The boy was quickly followed by Tyler. It was clear that the twin believed that if one of them could offer comfort, then two could offer twice as much.

Brady stood there for a moment, torn between letting them go and stopping them. He compromised by following the well-intentioned duo to Harper's room.

By the time he had reached it, the twins had already knocked on Harper's door and had gotten her to let them in.

Brady walked into Harper's room in time to see the sight of the nanny's opened suitcase stop the twins dead in their tracks. Something akin to shock registered on their expressive faces.

"Why are you packing up your things?" Tyler wanted to know.

"Are you going somewhere?" Toby asked, frowning at the suitcase.

A horror-stricken look came over Tyler's face as he asked, "Are you going away?"

Harper wasn't about to lie to the twins. "I'm going back to my apartment," she replied, placing a stack of blouses into the suitcase.

That just gave birth to a worse thought. "Are you leaving us?" Toby cried in disbelief.

Harper knew that Brady was watching her and it surprised her that he wasn't interfering or attempting to set the twins straight. Instead, he was leaving this all up to her.

She didn't know whether to feel grateful or feel abandoned.

For the time being, she decided to take the easy way out and just go along with the simplest explanation for her actions. To go into any explanation as to what she was really feeling was just too painful for her. She was afraid that she would start crying.

"Well, you're not sick anymore so you don't need me to be here every night, all night. I still have my apartment," she told them, which was true. Before she had accepted the position as their nanny, she had signed a short-term lease. It wasn't up yet and the landlord had refused to release her from the agreement—which now seemed like a good thing.

"Can't you get rid of it?" Toby wanted to know.

As she packed up the last of her things, she kept her answer simple. "Not really."

Toby's eyebrows knitted together in consternation. "Why?" he wanted to know.

This was harder than she had anticipated. "It's complicated," she answered.

Obviously that still didn't make any sense to the boy. "What does that mean?" he asked.

"It's what grown-ups say when they don't want to tell you something," Tyler, the more sensitive of the two, explained.

This was just going around in circles. It was time to wind the topic up. "I'll be back in the morning to make you breakfast," she promised the twins, zipping the suitcase and swinging it off the bed. "Probably before either one of you even wakes up."

Toby still looked skeptical. But Tyler just wanted something to hold on to. "You promise?" he asked her, looking up into her eyes.

"I promise," she answered without hesitation. "Now behave, both of you. And listen to your uncle Brady. I expect you to be good," she warned, adding, "I'll be back tomorrow for a full report," as she made her way down the stairs.

Setting the suitcase down, Harper extended the handle and pulled the luggage over to the door.

She wanted to pause and blow both boys a kiss, but she knew if she turned around to look at them, she wouldn't be able to make it out the front door. So she just kept going.

She was actually going through with it, Brady thought, watching Harper walk out. He really hadn't thought she would do it. He felt numb, like someone trapped in a bizarre dream, desperate to wake up.

"She left us," Toby cried, his voice vibrated in disbelief.

Tyler sighed heavily. "Everybody leaves us," he said sadly. "Mommy and Daddy left. Harper left and someday," he continued, turning to look at Brady before he said to Toby, "Unca Brady will leave us, too. 'Cause we're bad boys." His lower lip quivered. "Everybody says so."

That was when Brady realized that Tyler was crying and Toby was sniffling, doing his best *not* to cry.

The whole scene—and the declaration behind it—hit Brady like a powerful punch to the gut. He could remember his initial reaction when he found out that he had been appointed the twins' guardian. At the time all he had wanted to do was turn tail and run.

But at this moment, he realized that he didn't feel that way any longer. Somewhere along the line, without being aware of it, he had grown to love these two over-energized little boys. Love them fiercely with all his heart.

"Come here, guys," he said to them, sitting down on the sofa.

He drew the twins to him. For once, there was no jockeying for position, no fighting over who sat where. The twins just sank down on the sofa, one on either side of their "Unca" Brady.

Brady put one arm around each small boy and hugged the sad little soldiers to him.

"I'm not going to go anywhere," he told them. "And I will *always*, always be here to take care of you."

Tyler looked up at him. "You promise?"

"I promise," he told the twins, adding, "Even when you don't want me to."

"We'll always want you to," Tyler said solemnly, speaking for both himself and for Toby.

Though touched by the boy's serious expression, Brady could only laugh. "Remember saying that in ten or eleven years," he told the boy, knowing firsthand what teenage kids could be like.

"We'll remember," Tyler promised, nodding his head up and down.

"Yeah, we'll remember for a hundred years, not just eleven," Toby told Brady confidently.

The serious moment was lightened. *We'll see*, Brady thought, feeling his heart filling with love.

He continued sitting there with the twins, doing his best to offer them comfort and reassurance.

He also found himself thinking that maybe Harper had been right after all. The twins were getting too attached to her.

As for him, well, it was too late for him. He was attracted to Harper as well as attached and there was nothing he could do about it.

For whatever reason, she seemed to have some sort of emotional baggage weighing her down. She needed to deal with that before she could deal with anything else.

The way Brady saw it, it was in the best interests of everyone involved if he started to keep his distance from Harper. No matter how difficult that would be.

He believed her when she said she would be back in the morning and believed her when she said she intended to remain until he found someone to take her place. But even that wasn't going to be easy. He had been through interviews looking for a competent nanny before Harper ever came on the scene and *none* of the women he had spoken to even came *close* to holding a candle to her.

He had no reason to believe that things would be any different now than they had been when he had initially started his search. And after having Harper in their lives, he and the twins would just be settling for second best no matter who he hired.

Though he had low expectations, Brady made sure he put the word out that he would be interviewing nannies. If Harper was set on leaving, then it was best for all concerned if he ripped the Band-Aid off as soon as possible.

It was as arduous a task as he expected and his heart really wasn't in it, but he plowed through the interviews, talking to one woman after another. He finally settled on a middle-aged woman with two degrees in child psychology. Slightly heavyset, Sharon Overton had short, fluffy gray hair, thin lips and brown eyes. She seemed qualified and pleasant enough, but he felt she had no spark, no imagination.

Still, she was certainly better than the squadron of nannies he had already interviewed.

She just wasn't Harper, he silently admitted, but then, no one was.

The interview over, Mrs. Overton was set to

start as the twins' nanny at the beginning of April.

When it was finally decided, he told Harper. She received the news stoically.

He put his own interpretation to her behavior. "I know you didn't want to wait until then, but it's the soonest she can come on the job."

"I understand," Harper replied quietly. She could feel sadness flooding through her and did what she could to block the feeling. "In the interim," she continued, "we still have to get through Easter."

"You *are* coming with us to the big Easter egg hunt, right, Harper?" Tyler asked hopefully, watching her face.

"You said you would. You promised," Toby reminded her. "And we'll be on our best behavior," he declared, as if that would help to convince her.

"Well, I certainly can't resist an offer like that," Harper told the twins. "C'mon," she coaxed, "let's get the two of you dressed."

"And then can we help you get dressed?" Toby offered innocently.

"I can manage," she assured the boy with a wide smile. "But thank you. That was very thoughtful of you to offer." Moved, Harper kissed each of the boys on the top of his head.

Oh lord, she was going to miss them, she thought. Really miss them.

Harper felt a sadness fill her as she realized that this would probably be the last time the four of them would be together like this. April would be here in the blink of an eye and with April came the new nanny.

She told herself not to dwell on that.

Everything was going to work out for the best, she promised herself as they approached the Hotel Fortune.

"Oh boy, look at all these people!" Toby cried, his eyes growing wide as he glanced from one group to another. He didn't know where to look first. "Are they all gonna be hunting for Easter eggs?" he asked Harper. It was obvious that the idea worried him. "There won't be any eggs left," he lamented.

"Only the kids will be doing all the hunting for eggs," she told him with a wink. "Besides, you and your brother will probably outdo them all," she predicted with pride.

The twin puffed up his chest, as did his brother. "Yeah," he agreed gleefully.

The lobby of the hotel was crowded to over-flowing and moving around was a challenge. There was even a long line of patrons waiting to be seated at Roja. It seemed like everyone at Rambling Rose wanted to have brunch at the hotel, Harper thought. She was about to say as much to Brady when she suddenly spotted a familiar face.

The *last* face she wanted to see.

It was her old boss, Justine Wheeler, the soon-to-be ex-wife of the man Justine had accused her of having an affair with. The woman who had also angrily accused her of trying to wreck her marriage, a marriage that was already beyond repair.

Realizing she had stopped moving, Brady turned around to look at her.

"Is something wrong?" he asked Harper. "You suddenly look awfully pale. Are you feeling all right?" he wanted to know, concerned.

She grasped at the way out he had just handed her. "As a matter of fact, I'm not. Excuse me, please," she said and without any further explanation or waiting for Brady to respond, Harper quickly ducked into the ladies' room.

Startled, Tyler watched his nanny take off. "Where's Harper going?" he asked Brady.

"She's going to the ladies' room, Tyler," Brady told the boy.

Toby asked the question he had always heard put to him whenever he said he needed to go to the bathroom himself. "Why didn't she go at home?"

"Maybe she didn't think of it when she was home." Brady was still looking toward the ladies' room, wondering if he should be concerned. "Don't worry. I'm sure she'll be right back," he said for the twins' benefit. "Meanwhile, why don't we look around?" he suggested, ushering the twins toward where the egg hunt was soon to be held.

She knew she was hiding, but what choice did she have, Harper thought.

She stayed in the ladies' room longer than she wanted to, trying to figure out what to do.

By the time Megan Fortune came in, looking for her, Harper had decided that she needed to go home.

"Harper, are you all right?" Megan asked her, looking concerned. "Brady sent me," she explained. "He told me that he was worried about you. Should he be?"

She didn't have time to worry about Brady. She had a feeling all hell was going to break loose any moment now. "I need to go home, Megan," Harper blurted out. She felt like a mouse, trapped in a maze with no way out. "Coming here was a big mistake."

Megan looked at her, totally confused and not a little puzzled. "I don't understand. Why would coming here be a mistake?"

Harper was searching for a rational way to

explain this to Brady's cousin when Justine Wheeler chose that moment to walk in.

The second that the tall, thin well-dressed woman saw Harper, a condescending, nasty expression slid over her sharp features. The look in her eyes bordered on hatred.

"Well, well, well, look what the cat dragged in. Apparently the rumors that I heard were true," she said smugly. "I see that you're here, trying to sink your hooks into another one."

Megan was instantly protective and indignant at the tone this woman was using, not to mention what she was saying. "Now just hold on, lady. You can't talk to Harper that way," Brady's cousin declared angrily.

Justine raised her chin, her eyes turning into angry slits. "I can and I will. I see she had you fooled, but allow me to set you straight about this she-devil.

"Pollyanna here is a gold digger looking for her next sugar daddy. Aren't you, honey?" Justine asked condescendingly, smirking at Harper. "She swooped into my life, all phony sweetness and light, mesmerizing my husband who she decided was going to be her next victim. But I saw right through her and put an end to it. I fired *her*," the woman declared proudly, "and threw *his* ass out. Make sure she doesn't get near your man," Justine warned, "unless you're ready to lose him."

Harper wanted to defend herself, to put Justine in her place, but what was the point? The more she would protest the picture the hateful woman painted, the more tangled up the whole situation would become. Justine had already made up her mind about her and from the looks of it, she wasn't about to hesitate spreading these terrible lies about her.

She obviously seemed to relish it.

Feeling like she was suddenly suffocating, Harper raced out of the ladies' room.

"That's right, run away," Justine stood in the ladies' room doorway, shouting after her. "But you can't outrun the truth!"

The taunt echoed through the hallway.

Chapter Eighteen

Despite all the other people and their children milling around the hotel lobby, Brady saw Harper coming toward him across the floor. It concerned him that she looked even worse now than she had when she had gone running into the ladies' room.

"Harper, did Megan find you?" he questioned, then realized that she must have. "Is everything all right?" The woman was as white as a sheet. "You look like you've seen a ghost."

Harper didn't bother commenting on his observation. All she told him was, "I have to leave now, Brady. I just came looking for you so I could tell you that I was going."

"Now?" he asked, perplexed. The whole point of coming here was for the twins to take part in the egg hunt. It had been Harper's idea in the first place. That was why they had gone shopping for new Easter clothes. He knew the boys would be really disappointed if they wound up missing the hunt.

"Now," Harper answered. "I'll get a cab. You stay with the boys. I'll call you later and explain everything."

He still couldn't believe that she was leaving. She hadn't been that ill when they left the house. How had she gotten so sick so fast? "But—"

"C'mon, Unca Brady. We gotta go!" Toby insisted. He pointed to the giant, six-foot white bunny that was crossing the lobby and heading toward the garden. "They're gonna start the egg hunt," the twin cried eagerly, pulling on Brady's leg as he tried to get "Unca" Brady to follow him.

Brady found himself torn between being a good guardian and being there for Harper, who was obviously in some sort of pain.

He hadn't counted on something like this happening. "I—" he began.

Harper shook her head. "That's okay," she assured Brady. All she wanted to do right now was to get away. "You should go," she urged him.

To keep Brady from arguing any further, she

quickly hurried away from him as well as from the twins and headed straight for the hotel's main exit.

"C'mon, Unca Brady, let's go," Toby cried. "The bunny's getting away!"

Grabbing Brady's hand, Toby wrapped his small, sturdy fingers around it and began yanking him out into the hotel garden.

The hotel staff in charge of decorations had been working all week to turn the garden setting into an Easter wonderland for what promised to be the first annual egg hunt.

Brady had already lost sight of Harper. Well, at least the egg hunt would divert the twins from the fact that Harper had just taken off like that, he thought. He was doing his best to look on the bright side—if there actually was a bright side to all this.

"All right, let's go," he agreed, picking up his pace as he tried to keep up with the twins.

Harper managed to get to her apartment in record time. The moment she unlocked the door and walked in, it felt small to her, even for a studio. Almost claustrophobic, she realized. She found herself feeling trapped.

But she was not about to venture out again.

Not until she mentally made peace with what she assumed was taking place beyond her front door.

She had no doubt that her former employer

was out for revenge. Justine's vicious take on what she believed had happened between her nanny and her husband was undoubtedly all over the Hotel Fortune by now.

The thought of having to face that wall of hatred was almost more than Harper could bear. It felt practically suffocating to her. And the awful thing about the whole situation was that she had never done *anything* to encourage Justine's husband. Not once.

The only thing she had ever been guilty of was being polite and not telling Edward Wheeler what he could do with all his unwanted attention.

Maybe she should have, Harper thought now. But it would have done no good.

Struggling to calm down, Harper took out her cell phone and placed it on the tiny coffee table in front of her so she could quickly pick it up when it rang.

It didn't ring.

Fifteen minutes went by. She decided that Brady *wasn't* going to call.

Well, she supposed that she couldn't really blame the man. When she had fled the hotel ladies' room, Justine's voice had been ringing in her ears. The woman had been extremely passionate in her diatribe. By now, everyone at the hotel's Easter festivities knew what Justine *believed* had happened.

Harper convinced herself that she was better off leaving.

No one should have to deal with those kind of lies.

"My lord, Brady, you should have heard that witch shrieking and carrying on," Megan told her cousin after she had finally found him. The moment she did, she quickly reported, in a nutshell, the reason she felt that Harper had taken off the way she had. "I would have left the shrew, too, if I were her husband." Just thinking about what had been said made Megan shiver. "That witch accused Harper of the most awful things! Things I *know* she couldn't have done," Megan said loyally. "Harper is just too good a person to have done any of those things."

It was all coming together now and making sense, Brady thought, listening to what his cousin was telling him. He understood now why Harper had been so distressed about her former employer—and why she wouldn't talk about it.

Harper had never struck him as a woman who spoke ill about someone, no matter how much they might deserve it. Still, he felt that she should have come to him about it. He would have listened to her and more important, he would have believed her and helped her deal with it.

As Megan said, Harper was just too nice. He,

on the other hand, knew how to handle vicious, mean-spirited people.

Momentarily turning away from the twins, Brady told his cousin that he appreciated having her go after Harper. "And thanks for telling me all this," he said, taking out his cell phone. There was no question in his mind that he needed to clear all this up and get Harper to come back. She needed to know that he didn't believe any of the lies the Wheeler woman was telling. "I have to call Harper and—"

The rest of what he was about to tell his cousin was cut short when they, as well as everyone around them, heard the awful scream.

Brady swung around to find that Toby, who had been running around the garden only a second ago, was flat on his back at the base of one of the trees.

He, Megan and Tyler, not to mention a number of other people, instantly ran over to the screaming boy.

"What happened?" Brady cried, stunned. How could this have happened? He had only looked away from Toby for a minute.

Maybe less.

Stunned, Toby could only cry in pain. Tyler quickly filled them all in. "Toby climbed up that tree." He pointed up to one of the higher branches. "He thought there were Easter eggs in that nest up there."

Tyler's explanation was drowned out by a fresh wave of Toby's screams. "My arm! It hurts, it hurts," the boy sobbed.

"I'll call an ambulance," Megan told her cousin. She looked sympathetically at Toby as she waited for her 9-1-1 call to go through. "Hang in there, Toby," she encouraged the boy.

Brady couldn't help it. He looked anxiously around the gathered crowd, hoping against hope that he'd see Harper making her way toward them. But he knew better. This was now the new normal, which meant that he was going to have to handle this situation without her.

He knelt down beside Toby and reassured him. But it was Tyler who shifted nervously from foot to foot. "Is he going to die?" he asked Brady, terrified.

Brady took the boy's hands in his. "Nobody's going to die, Tyler," Brady told him as calmly as he could, secretly relieved that he was able to say that to him. "Toby's going to be just fine."

As the sound of an approaching ambulance pierced the ongoing commotion, he wished he could say the same for himself.

"I'm afraid that the boy's arm is broken, Mr. Fortune," the young emergency-room physician told him after he had looked at the X-rays that had been taken of Toby's injuries. "Frankly, considering that Toby fell out of that tree, he's very lucky that his arm is the only thing he broke."

"I don't feel lucky," Toby complained. "It hurts!"

The physician, Dr. Neubert, looked sympathetically at the little boy. "I'm sure it does, but the good news is it's a clean break and considering how young Toby is," he told Brady, "it should heal fast." He smiled at Toby. "You'll be back to running around in no time," Dr. Neubert assured him.

Despite the positive news, Brady could see that Toby was doing his best not to cry.

The twin's lower lip quivered as he looked at him and said, "I want Harper, Unca Brady."

It killed him to have to tell the boy, "I'm afraid Harper's not here, Toby."

"Where is she?" Tyler piped up, ready to go looking for the nanny if it would make his brother feel better—because that would make him feel better, too.

Brady glanced at Megan, who had driven Tyler in his car to the hospital while he rode with Toby in the ambulance. He really didn't want to talk about this right now but Megan silently encouraged him. "Harper's home, Tyler."

"Home?" Tyler echoed, confused. "What's she

doing home?" he wanted to know. It didn't make sense to him. Toby needed her. She was always there when they needed her.

"She wasn't feeling well," Brady answered, sounding a little short. He saw Tyler's face fall and immediately felt bad as he apologized. "I'm worried about your brother, too, Ty. Why don't you keep him company for a minute? I want to talk to the doctor about something."

"About Harper not feeling well?" Tyler questioned.

Going on with life after Harper if he couldn't convince her to come back wasn't going to be easy, Brady thought. But that was something he would tackle later. The immediate thing was making sure that Toby received the proper care.

"No," he told the twin, "about Toby. I'll be right back," he promised as he stepped away. "Dr. Neubert," he called out to the ER physician, "I want to ask you a question." He stepped out into the hallway, the doctor following him.

Brady was in such a hurry to talk to the busy doctor, he didn't realize that he had left his cell phone on the chair next to Tyler.

But Tyler spotted it immediately.

Megan was in the small, curtained exam room with them. Right now she was talking to Toby. Taking advantage of her inattention, Tyler quickly put his hand over his uncle's cell phone and moved over to the furthest corner of the room. He turned his back to his brother and Megan.

Brady had left his cell phone unlocked. Tyler and his brother had cut their eyeteeth on cell phones, frequently playing games on their parents' and then Brady's phones when he let them. And he'd watched his uncle make enough calls that he knew exactly what to do. Tyler hit the folder icon for Contacts and scrolled through the names. Now he was grateful that Harper had worked with him and Toby to learn to write all their names. He recognized the name he was looking for.

Harper's.

Thinking that his "unca" would be back at any second, Tyler hit the little green arrow. He listened to the phone on the other end ring.

Harper saw Brady's name and number pop up. The second it did, her heart began pounding. She still had no idea what she was going to tell him, but right now, all that mattered to her was that Brady *was* calling.

"Hello?" she said uncertainly.

"Harper?"

That wasn't Brady.

For a second, the sound of the childish voice

on the other end threw her, not to mention that she was incredibly disappointed.

Brady wasn't calling her. One of the twins was. "Tyler?" she guessed because he was the more subdued one of the duo. "Honey, why are you calling me? Where's your uncle Brady?"

"We're in the hospital, Harper," Tyler told her, distress vibrating in his voice.

Harper's mind instantly began racing as all sorts of scenarios occurred to her. Her stomach tightened. "What are you doing in the hospital?"

"There was an accident, Harper," the boy blurted out. "Unca Brady needs you. Please come," he begged.

"Tyler? What kind of an accident?" Harper asked the boy. "Tyler?"

The only thing she heard in response to her questions was a dial tone.

Stunned, she stared at the cell phone.

An accident.

Harper's hand was trembling as she put her cell phone back in her pocket.

Her heart was pounding hard in her chest as she got her purse and found her car keys. Terrifying realizations filtered through her mind.

If one of the twins was calling her, that meant that Brady wasn't able to call himself.

Oh lord, had that horrible woman sought him out? Had Brady been so upset, so mad that he'd gotten into an accident after hearing Justine call her all those awful names?

What if he had been driving home with the kids and— A horrible chill went down her spine as she thought about Brady and the twins being hurt—or worse.

What if in Brady's case it *had* been worse?

He had to be unconscious because if he wasn't, why would Tyler be calling her instead of Brady?

What if it was worse than being unconscious, her mind posed.

What if—?

"Oh please don't let him die," she cried out loud as she raced to her car.

Harper didn't remember driving to the hospital. All she remembered was praying, as she flew through the lights, that she wasn't too late.

Nothing else mattered except that.

Brady couldn't die, Harper kept thinking over and over. He couldn't die.

She didn't remember parking her car. All she was aware of was running and praying.

Her heart in her throat, she asked the woman at the reception desk if a Brady Fortune had been brought into the hospital in the last few hours.

"Fortune, Fortune," the young brunette muttered under her breath as she scrolled through the list of names of the people who had been seen in the emergency room in the last few hours. "No, no Brady Fortune," she told Harper, looking up. "But there was a Toby Fortune brought in a while ago," she said. "They're still in the ER. I can—"

The receptionist didn't get a chance to finish. Harper was already running to the double doors that divided the ER from the rest of the first floor.

"You can't just go in there like that," the receptionist proclaimed, standing up so her voice would carry.

Harper only heard the woman as just so much background noise, barely paying attention to what she said.

He wasn't dead. Brady wasn't dead.

Those words beat like a refrain, over and over again, in her brain.

He wasn't dead.

But what was Toby doing in the ER?

All sorts of concerns crowded her brain.

She had no idea which exam room Toby and Brady was in, but she was prepared to go into each and every one until she either found them or they dragged her away.

But as it turned out, she didn't have to do either.

As soon as she stepped into the ER, she saw Brady standing in the hallway outside a room, talking to a nurse.

She didn't hear what they were saying. She

didn't *care* what they were saying. All that mattered was that Brady was there, standing up and talking.

He hadn't been hurt.

"Brady!" Harper cried half a beat before she threw herself, sobbing, into his arms. "You're not dead!"

He had no idea what to make of the emotional display or where she might have gotten the idea that he was dead. All he knew was that Harper was here, in his arms, and she had never felt so good to him as she did right at this moment.

He only realized that she was sobbing as he continued holding her.

Chapter Nineteen

Tyler threw his arms around her leg and wiggled in between Harper and Brady. "Harper, you came!" he cried excitedly.

"Hey, me, too!" Toby piped up, unable to reach Harper from his bed, but there was no way he wanted to be left out. "I'm the one who fell out of the tree!" the twin complained.

Wiping away her tears, she entered the room and embraced Toby, careful not to touch his cast. She knew that could wind up hurting the boy. "You don't have to tell me," she assured him. "I know that—and don't you ever do that to me again," she warned him. "I was worried sick."

"No, no more flying squirrel tricks for him,"

Brady declared, looking directly at the injured twin. "Right, Toby?"

"Don't worry, Unca Brady. I learned my lesson good," the boy told him solemnly.

Brady sighed as he rolled his eyes. "Oh, if only I could believe that."

"I really mean it, Unca Brady," Toby vowed, awkwardly crossing his heart with his left hand.

Twisting around to look up at Harper, who had stepped back and was leaning against Brady, Tyler hopefully asked, "Are you gonna go home with us, Harper?"

With all her heart, she really wanted to. But she had actually resigned from the position and Brady had hired someone else to take her place, so it was all out of her hands now.

"That's up to your uncle Brady," Harper said.

Tyler turned to face his guardian now. "Can she come home with us, Unca Brady?"

"Yeah, can she? Pleeeease?" Toby asked, adding his voice to the entreaty.

Brady was with the twins on this, but he didn't want to pressure Harper into agreeing to anything. "Sure. But only if she wants to."

"Do ya, Harper?" Tyler asked eagerly.

Toby gave her the most pathetic look as he echoed Tyler. "Do ya?"

Harper grinned broadly at the two boys. "Just try and stop me."

"Nobody's gonna stop you, Harper," Toby guaranteed. "Right, Unca Brady?"

Brady smiled as his eyes met Harper's. "Right," he agreed.

Brady brought his vehicle directly up to the hospital entrance as Harper stood to the side. She was holding on to Toby's wheelchair while Tyler waved madly at Brady just in case he didn't see them.

Toby was ready to break into a run and wasn't happy about being restrained in the wheelchair this way. "I broke my arm, not my leg. Why do I gotta sit in this stupid wheelchair?" he wanted to know.

"It's hospital policy, Toby," Harper told the boy. "You don't want to make anyone unhappy by breaking the rules now, do you?"

Toby hung his head and sighed. "No, ma'am."

She patted the arm that wasn't in a cast. "Good boy," she praised, just as Brady brought his vehicle to a stop before them.

"Ready?" he asked Toby, getting out.

"Oh, so ready," Toby declared with enthusiasm. "I just wanna go home with Harper."

Brady glanced in her direction and said, "Me, too."

Harper's heart warmed and swelled.

The next moment Harper secured Tyler into

his car seat while Brady did the same with Toby, lifting the injured twin because he was able to handle the heavy cast more easily than Harper. But when it came to securing the car-seat straps, Toby spoke up, asking that Harper do it. He even added "Please" to clinch his request.

"I'd be happy to," Harper told the twin.

Tyler leaned over, watching Harper as she finished securing his brother in the car seat. "I guess we're all back together again," Tyler announced happily.

"It certainly looks that way," Brady answered. "I can come by with one of my brothers and we can bring your car to the house later," he told Harper. Right now he knew it was important for Toby to be assured that Harper was coming home with them.

Getting into the front seat behind the steering wheel, Brady glanced at Harper as he started up the car. He couldn't begin to put into words how happy he was to have her here with them now.

After turning on the engine, he pulled out of the parking lot.

The words burned on her tongue. Harper couldn't keep this to herself any longer. She leaned in toward Brady so her voice wouldn't carry to the backseat as she told him, "I really tried to fight this, to stay away, but I just simply can't." She flushed, embarrassed, thinking of what had transpired earlier today. "I can only imagine what you might think of me."

He knew what she was talking about. "I only heard a little bit from Megan about what happened before Toby fell out of the tree." But then, he didn't need to hear everything. "Why on earth would you think that I would take that woman's word over yours?"

Harper shrugged. She couldn't really explain it. "I was just afraid, that's all. People tend to believe the worst."

"I don't," he told her simply.

She glanced over her shoulder at the duo behind them, but the twins, thanks to the extremely emotionally trying day they had both put in, were exhausted and had already fallen asleep.

Satisfied that the twins wouldn't overhear her, Harper turned around to face Brady. It was time that he heard the truth.

"I didn't realize what was going on at first but it turned out that Justine's husband began paying unwanted attention to me almost from the beginning. And he started complimenting me. First about the way I was handling his daughters, then about the way I looked and dressed.

"I thought maybe I was imagining things, but then he would find ways to corner me. I knew for a fact that he was seeing other women behind his wife's back and he tried more than once to add me to the pack. I needed the job—especially after Justine accepted a job transfer to Rambling Rose and talked me into coming with them. She said she couldn't take care of her children and handle the rigors of working on a new job. She made me feel that I would be abandoning her if I left, so I agreed to come with the family and didn't say anything about the way her husband was behaving."

Harper sighed, remembering. Wishing she didn't. "I just kept trying to avoid Edward—until Justine walked in on us and misunderstood my pushing Edward away as some sort of foreplay. She became livid, called me all sorts of names and fired me on the spot. She also said she was going to see to it that I would never work as a nanny again, here or anywhere else. Ever," Harper emphasized. "Justine had such an authoritative way about her, I was sure everyone would believe her."

Brady blew out a breath, shaking his head. "That's what bullies count on. That they can intimidate you. I'm sorry you had to go through that—and sorry that you *ever* thought I would take her side instead of yours," he concluded.

It all felt like a horrible nightmare now. "I never wanted you to find out and I *never* wanted you and the boys to suffer because of me," she told him.

Brady nodded. "I have to admit, when you first said that, that you needed space between us, I thought you were right." Glancing at her, he saw surprise flicker in her eyes. "That I needed to focus on the twins. I didn't feel that I had any business getting involved with you—or anyone right now—because of this whole situation with the twins. But it's too late. I love you," he told her. As she stared at him, dumbfounded, he went on to say, "The kids love you as well and to be honest, I believe that we're all better off together. You can see that, can't you?" he asked, searching her face.

Her mouth dropped open. She was utterly surprised at the depth of the feelings that Brady had just expressed. Feelings that were entirely mutual.

He had just poured out his heart to her and she hadn't made a single comment. He didn't know what to make of it. "Say something," he told her.

He had managed to take her breath away and she searched for the words to explain her silence and how she felt about what he had just said.

"I didn't think you were interested in a serious relationship," she confessed.

"I wasn't," he answered honestly. "I never expected *any* of this. It just happened. But when it's right," he went on, pulling up into his driveway and turning off the engine to look at her, "it's right. And this," he concluded, drawing her into his arms, "is so *very* right."

Glancing behind him, he saw that the twins were still asleep. So Brady kissed her.

Long and hard.

"I think," he said some moments later, "that should put an end to all the arguments."

She smiled up into his eyes. "At least for now."

There was a lightness within her. A lightness she hadn't thought she would ever be able to experience again, especially after everything that had happened recently.

It felt *wonderful*.

"Does this mean you're really gonna stay, Harper?" came a sleepy voice from the backseat.

Startled, they turned and looked at Tyler. "Hey, I thought you were supposed to be asleep, big guy," Brady said to the boy.

"I woke up," Tyler said, executing a yawn that was bigger than he was.

"So I see," Brady told the twin with a laugh.

Tyler turned to look at Harper. Nobody had answered his question yet. "So are you really gonna stay?" he asked Harper again, then before she could answer, he added, "Please say yes. If you do, it'll make Toby get better real fast," he promised.

"Well, I certainly can't argue with that," she

told the twin. Because he was still waiting, she answered, "Yes, Tyler, I'm going to stay."

But Tyler was still leery and he wasn't completely convinced. "For a long time?" he wanted to know.

"Yes, for a *very* long time," she answered.

"Yay," he cheered. At the same time, he was desperately fighting to keep his eyes open.

"I hope she plans on staying forever," Brady told the boy as he looked at Harper.

For her part, Harper was totally stunned to hear Brady say that. After everything that had happened, she hadn't expected that. "Do you mean it?" she asked him.

"I never meant anything more in my entire life," he replied. "There's a vacant position at the boys' school. I'm sure that the nanny I just hired to take your place—by the way, nobody can take your place—would be happy to transfer there.

"I realize that it might sound like I'm moving a little fast here," he allowed, "but I've already been dragging my feet too long and it's about time I started taking steps that were moving in the right direction—for everyone." He looked into her eyes, searching for a sign that she understood. "Am I making myself clear?" he asked her, afraid that his meaning was getting lost amid the myriad of words that had come spilling out of him just now.

Harper laughed helplessly. "Right now, my head is spinning around with all sorts of thoughts that are chasing each other," she confessed.

"Tell you what. Why don't we take these guys inside and I can try to make myself clearer after we put the twins to bed?" he told her hopefully.

Her eyes smiled at him. "Sounds good to me," she replied.

After getting out of the vehicle, they each took a twin. Harper carried Tyler while Brady had Toby in his arms and brought the boy into the house, careful not to jostle his cast. The last thing he wanted was to cause Toby pain and wake him up.

Harper realized that she still had the keys to Brady's house on her. Tucking Tyler against her shoulder, she reached into her pocket and got the keys out, then unlocked the front door. Holding it open with her back, she allowed Brady to come in and carry Toby slowly up to the room he shared with Tyler.

Harper was right behind them, moving almost in slow motion even though every fiber in her body was urging her to bring the boy into his room as quickly as possible so that she would be free to finally be alone with Brady. She wanted to be able to clear the rest of the air as soon as possible.

But that all involved her own needs, and her

needs, no matter what they were, did not take precedence over the twins' needs. She had lost sight of that for a little bit, Harper now realized, and that sort of thing could never be allowed to happen again.

Tyler moaned a little when she gently placed him down on his bed.

"Shhh, Tyler," she whispered to him. "Go back to sleep. You need your rest so that you can be there to help your brother tomorrow."

Tyler made a noise in response and it sounded as if he thought he was answering her.

Harper smiled down at him. "That's my boy," she coaxed. "Go back to sleep. I'm just going to take these clothes off so you can curl up under your blanket, okay, little man?" She was saying everything in a singsong voice meant to lull Tyler back to sleep.

He cooperated.

Harper finally managed to get Tyler undressed and comfortably lying back in his bed. She covered him with the blanket.

Raising her eyes to Brady's, she nodded toward Tyler and murmured, "Okay, one down, one to go."

Brady looked a little uncertainly at Toby. With his cast, he looked so terribly vulnerable to him right now. "Are you sure you want to undress Toby?" he asked her.

"You want to put him to bed in his clothes?" Harper asked, surprised.

"Well, given the circumstances, I'd rather do that than risk waking him up so that we get him into his pajamas. In this case, I think it's more important to let him sleep than to get him out of his Easter outfit." Having stated his case, Brady looked at her quizzically. "How about you?"

Smiling, she nodded her head. "My kid brother who would totally agree with you. As a matter of fact, he would be on your side even if you said that Toby should get to fall asleep in his street clothes every night."

"You don't talk about him often," Brady observed. He took her filling in the blanks as a sign that she was finally beginning to trust him. "You said he's in the army. Do you miss him?"

She was intent on carefully taking off Toby's shoes and socks. Finished, she placed them both neatly on the floor.

"Absolutely," she said with feeling, "My brother was kind of wild when he was a kid. The complete opposite of me. He was always getting into things, exploring." She smiled, remembering. "Jack took off right after high school and wound up enlisting in the army. Right now, he's going from one base to another, seeing the world and being as happy as the proverbial clam." Her smile widened as fond memories crowded in her head. "He's living life the way he always dreamed," she told Brady.

"And you?" Brady asked. "What is it that you always wanted?"

She secured Toby's blanket, making sure he remained covered. "To be exactly where I am," she told him. "Being the boys' nanny."

"Like I said when you first came to work here, taking care of the twins, I don't know how I got so lucky, but I know better than to question my good fortune—and theirs." The corners of his mouth quirked in an amused smile as the word replayed itself in his head. "You should only pardon the pun."

Her eyes crinkled as she stepped back, away from the boy's beds, and moved closer to the door. "I will if you will," she told him.

"Do you want to go into your room and have that talk now?" he asked Harper.

Harper looked over her shoulder. The twins were both asleep. With any luck, they would continue sleeping until morning.

"I think it's safe to leave them now," she whispered to Brady.

"Okay, then," Brady replied, gesturing toward the doorway. "Lead the way."

Chapter Twenty

The moment she walked into the room and heard the door close behind her, something told Harper that this time, it was going to be different.

A warm shiver shimmied down her spine and then her skin heated as she turned around to face Brady.

Her breath caught in her throat as he cupped her face in his hands.

"I don't need any explanations, Harper," he told her quietly.

Her mouth felt dry as she tried to talk. "Are you sure? Because I feel like I owe you one," Harper told Brady.

The space between them had managed to

grow smaller. "You don't owe me anything," he assured her. "Just always know that I'll have your back, no matter what," he said just before he brought his mouth down on hers.

The moment he did, Harper could feel it. She could feel a tidal wave suddenly swelling up and then washing over her with incredible power until every single part of her was drenched.

Her heart pounding like a giant timpani, Harper threw her arms around his neck, totally submerging herself in his kiss.

She didn't attempt to fight it. There was no point to even trying. No point in pretending that this wasn't what she had been wanting all along, right from the very first moment she had met him.

She gloried in the feel of his lips against hers, the oh-so-tantalizing feel of his hands as they moved slowly along her skin, claiming her.

His touch aroused her to such heights that she could hardly breathe, growing more and more dizzy.

Within moments, they were no longer standing next to the locked door in her room. Somehow, they had moved over and were now on her bed, urgently pressed against one another, desperately absorbing the feel of their bodies as heat radiated from each of them, merging into a giant flame that was only growing in size and scope.

Each kiss just fed on the next, creating an urgent desire for more. The passion between them mounted, increasing with each passing second.

The urgency of the desire between them grew more demanding.

All she could think of was splaying her hands and running her palms along his hard chest. But his shirt was in the way, fighting her. Harper almost ripped off two of his buttons in her desire to get the barrier out of her way.

Intent on getting them undone as fast as possible, she began to tug at the placket.

"Wait," Brady urged, then quickly unbuttoned the rest of his shirt. He stripped it from his torso and tossed the shirt aside without even glancing in its direction.

All that mattered was Harper, nothing else.

The moment the shirt was gone, Harper slid her hands over his chest. It was smooth and hard beneath her fingers.

Her breathing grew shorter, faster.

She began to tug off her own blouse. His hands moved hers away, then finished what she had started.

His eyes skimmed over her, touching her everywhere.

After that, who did what to whom became a blur. All she knew was that the rest of their clothing wound up flying off and then mingling on the floor when they finally landed.

And then their activity grew even hotter and more passionate, as well as more urgent.

Harper felt as if he was worshipping her with his hands. The second Brady began touching her, she just found herself wanting more and more.

There was no end to her desire, no satiation looming on the horizon.

She just wanted *more*.

Brady hadn't expected the sweet young woman to turn into such a wildcat, although there was a part of him that secretly suspected that this was bubbling, brewing just beneath the surface.

With each kiss they shared, his desire grew more demanding. Even with all the women he had known in his life, Harper had turned out to be a revelation.

The more he familiarized himself with her, the more he wanted to.

Their bodies completely nude and heated now, Brady reveled and feasted on each tempting curve before him, feeling as if he would never be able to satisfy his hunger for her.

But he gave it his best shot.

His mouth forged a network of hot, moist kisses up and down her supple, heaving body.

To his surprise, just as he was about to culminate his sensual journey and take her, Harper suddenly flipped around and began doing the very same thing to him, causing Brady's pulse to quicken erotically. His desire grew to such incredible heights, he didn't think he could hold himself in check too much longer.

In fact, he was certain of it.

So when she feathered her fingertips along his thighs, he caught her by the wrist and then drew her hand to his lips.

Why a kiss pressed to the palm of her hand could feel so sensually erotic was beyond her— but it did. So much so that she found that she was having trouble keeping her hands off him, trouble keeping her desire from exploding and drenching both of them.

Their bodies came together like two halves of a powerful magnet. They moved urgently against one another, heating until they all but incinerated.

And still the dance continued.

His mouth urgently slanting over hers, Brady finally took her.

He entered her slowly despite the urgency he could feel burning in his body. It was all he could do to prolong the ecstasy that hovered just beyond the perimeter, waiting to seize him.

The final moment hovered, about to explode. Her breath lodged within her throat.

And then she began to move, duplicating the ever-growing rhythm she felt throbbing within her.

They went faster and faster, moving to a tune that only they could hear beating and pulsing within them, growing ever louder until it completely claimed them. Taking them to the highest peak and then, finally, propelling them over the edge.

The heated vortex was waiting to seize them, making them one.

The sensation that had been created vibrated all through Harper, holding her in its grip until it finally began to fade. It slipped further and further into the distance.

And then it became part of the air.

Harper took in a deep breath, trying to steady her pulse, her quivering body. Finally it began to settle down and she nestled against him.

"That was some 'talk,'" she murmured.

Brady laughed, his arm tightening around her. "Remind me to have those talks with you more often."

She felt her smile spreading out to every part of her, completely lighting her up. "Oh, I'll remind you," she promised.

Brady had every intention of slipping out of her room once their lovemaking was over.

Harper needed her rest and he didn't want the boys to accidentally find them together this way.

Even so, he wanted to linger.

Just a little longer, he promised himself, holding her to him. All he wanted was just a little while longer, and then he would go.

The night somehow was able to get away from him. Neither one of them seemed to actually mind.

He made it out and to his own room just before the twins woke up.

This became the recurring theme defining their nights together from then on.

They didn't plan on it; it just seemed to happen. And Brady and Harper accepted it without any need for further discussion.

Each morning that Brady woke up next to Harper, he counted himself as one of the luckiest men on the face of the earth.

The more it happened, the more he knew that he never wanted that to change.

As Dr. Neubert, the ER physician, had predicted, Toby's arm healed without any incident and before long, the hyperactive twin was back to being his former self.

Added to that, Brady had filed papers to formally adopt the twins, officially making them a family.

Life was good. Very good.

Brady and Harper continued to end their nights in each other's arms, but Harper was determined that the twins wouldn't accidentally walk in on them together, so she made certain that Brady would go back to his bedroom before the twins were up.

But then, one morning, Brady seemed to slip up. He was still lying next to a drowsy Harper when she heard a knock on her door.

Before she could scramble up and get out of bed, the twins came barging in. Harper found herself wildly grateful that she and Brady were at least wearing their pajamas.

That wasn't always the case.

Gathering herself together as best she could, she realized that Tyler was carrying in a breakfast tray, one that looked precariously close to having its contents tumble to the floor.

"What are you guys doing here?" she asked. Glancing at Brady, she caught herself thinking that he was a better actor than she'd given him credit for. He looked as if he was taking the twins' unexpected appearance in stride. "Is everything okay?" she asked the boys. She was never too complacent when it came to the twins' behavior.

"Yeah! We brought you breakfast in bed," Toby

announced, looking at Brady with a wide smile. He had just recently gotten rid of his hated cast.

"So I see," Harper said. At least they weren't asking questions about finding Brady in her bed, she thought, taking solace in that. "What's the occasion?" she wanted to know.

"No occasion," Tyler answered in a higher voice than usual—and then he started to giggle.

Brady grabbed the tray before it could wind up on the bed or the floor.

Harper focused on what was actually *on* the tray. "Are those Pop-Tarts?" she asked Tyler.

"Uh-huh. I put jelly on them," Tyler proudly told her.

"And I brought the jelly beans and put them on the plates," Toby said, not to be excluded.

She had no idea what they were up to, but nonetheless she was delighted to take part in this unique family scenario.

"Well, it all looks delicious," she told the twins, forcing a smile to her lips. "I can't wait to dig in."

"Did you guys remember to bring the dessert?" Brady asked them.

"Dessert, too?" Harper repeated, amazed. "I'll be surprised if we don't go into some sort of a sugar coma," she told Brady.

Brady didn't comment on her observation. He

was watching Tyler, the more reliable twin, run out of the room.

The boy was back in a flash carrying a small bakery box. He brought it over to Harper and placed it on her lap.

"Open it, Harper," he urged.

"Yeah, open it," Toby cried, his eyes dancing.

"I will," she promised. "After I have the Pop-Tarts and the jelly beans."

"I think they want you to open it now," Brady told her.

That was odd. She looked at him quizzically. What was going on here?

"You know what they say," Brady told her. "You never know what could happen, so eat dessert first."

Since having her eat what was inside the box seemed to mean so much to all three of them, Harper gamely said, "Okay" and then opened the box.

There was no dessert in the pastry box.

Instead, Harper stared, stunned, at the small white box that was nestled in the center. Taking it out, she opened the white box to find a velvet box inside it.

As she opened that, she saw the most beautiful diamond ring she had ever seen sparkling inside it.

She looked up at Brady surrounded by the boys, their grins huge.

"Will you marry us?" Brady and the twins cried in unison.

Tears slid down her cheeks. It took her a moment to find her voice and then reply, with wholehearted enthusiasm, "Yes, oh yes, I will marry you. All three of you!" she declared, beaming at them.

The next moment, she found herself hugged by the twins, just before their "unca" Brady kissed her, amid their enthusiastic applause, to seal the deal.

The twins applauded for a long time.

* * * * *

*Look for the next book in the new
Harlequin Special Edition continuity
The Fortunes of Texas: The Hotel Fortune*
Runaway Groom
by Lynne Marshall

*On sale April 2021 wherever Harlequin books
and ebooks are sold.*

*And catch up with the previous
Fortunes of Texas titles:*

Her Texas New Year's Wish
by Michelle Major

Their Second-Time Valentine
by Helen Lacey

Available now!

**WE HOPE YOU ENJOYED
THIS BOOK FROM**

HARLEQUIN
SPECIAL
EDITION

Believe in love. Overcome obstacles. Find happiness.

Relate to finding comfort and strength in the
support of loved ones and enjoy the journey
no matter what life throws your way.

6 NEW BOOKS AVAILABLE EVERY MONTH!

COMING NEXT MONTH FROM

H HARLEQUIN
SPECIAL EDITION

Available March 30, 2021

#2827 RUNAWAY GROOM
The Fortunes of Texas: The Hotel Fortune • by Lynne Marshall
When Mark Mendoza discovers his fiancée cheating on him on their wedding day, he hightails it out of town. Megan Fortune is there to pick up the pieces—and to act as his faux girlfriend when his ex shows up. Mark swears he will never get involved again. Megan doesn't want to be a "rebound" fling. But they find each other irresistible. What's a fake couple to do?

#2828 A NEW FOUNDATION
Bainbridge House • by Rochelle Alers
While restoring a hotel with his adoptive siblings, engineer Taylor Williamson hires architectural historian Sonja Ríos-Martin. Neither of them ever thought they'd mix business with pleasure, but when their relationship runs into both of their pasts, they'll have to figure out if this passion is worth fighting for.

#2829 WYOMING MATCHMAKER
Dawson Family Ranch • by Melissa Senate
Divorced real estate agent Danica Dunbar still isn't ready for marriage and motherhood. When she has to care for her infant niece, Ford Dawson, the sexy detective who wants to settle down, is a little too helpful. Will this matchmaker pawn him off on someone else? Or is she about to make a match of her own?

#2830 THE RANCHER'S PROMISE
Match Made in Haven • by Brenda Harlen
Mitchell Gilmore was best man at Lindsay Delgado's wedding, "uncle" to her children and, when Lindsay is tragically widowed, a consoling shoulder. Until one electric kiss changes everything. Now Mitchell is determined to move from lifelong friendship to forever family. It's a risky proposition, but maybe Lindsay will finally make good on her promise.

#2831 THE TROUBLE WITH PICKET FENCES
Lovestruck, Vermont • by Teri Wilson
A pregnant former beauty queen and a veteran fire captain at the end of his rope realize it's never too late to build a family and that life, love and lemonade are sweeter when you let down your guard and open your heart to fate's most unexpected twists and turns.

#2832 THEIR SECOND-CHANCE BABY
The Parent Portal • by Tara Taylor Quinn
Annie Morgan needs her ex-husband's help—specifically, she needs him to sign over his rights to the embryos they had frozen prior to their divorce. But when she ends up pregnant—with twins—it becomes very clear their old feelings never left. Will their previous problems wreck their relationship once again?

HSECNM0321

"Do you want coffee?" Lindsay asked.

"No, thanks."

"So…how was your date?"

Considering that it was over before nine o'clock, she was surprised when Mitchell said, "Actually, it was great. It turns out that Karli's not just beautiful but smart and witty and fun. We had a great dinner and interesting conversation."

She didn't particularly want to hear all the details, but she'd been the one to insist they remain firmly within the friend zone and, as a friend, it was her duty to listen.

"That is great," she said. Lied. "I'm happy for you." Another lie. "But I have to wonder, if she's so great… why are you here?"

"Because she's not you," he said simply. "And I don't want anyone but you."

She might have resisted the words, but the intensity and sincerity of his gaze sent them arrowing straight to her heart. Still, she had to be smart. To think about what was at stake.

"I know you're afraid to risk our friendship, and I understand why. But there's so much more we could have together. So much more we could be to one another. Don't we deserve a chance to find out?"

Before Lindsay could respond to either his confession or his question, he was kissing her.